THE LAST OF THE COUNTRY HOUSE MURDERS

THE LAST OF THE COUNTRY HOUSE MURDERS

by Emma Tennant

THOMAS NELSON INC., PUBLISHERS
Nashville / New York

No character in this book is intended to represent any actual person; all the incidents of the story are entirely fictional in nature.

 Published by Thomas Nelson Inc., Publishers, Nashville, Tennessee. Manufactured in the United States of America.

First U.S. edition

Library of Congress Cataloging in Publication Data

Tennant, Emma.
The last of the country house murders.

I. Title.
PZ4.T288Las3 [PR6070.E52] 823'.9'14 76-6976
ISBN 0-8407-6490-1

For Tim

Contents

THE LAST OF THE COUNTRY HOUSE MURDERS

1

Woodiscombe Manor

"And there through the trees," said the guide in the blue uniform and scarlet armband, "there, ladies and gentlemen, is Woodiscombe Manor, the last country house." He paused for effect, and the tourists twisted sideways in their seats, pressing their faces against the glass of the bus windows so that from outside they looked like the rubber cakes displayed by the once-rich in their living quarters. There was a stir of excitement.

"Woodiscombe Manor," intoned the guide, "was built of red brick in the sixteenth century, the gray stone facade was added in the eighteenth, turrets and gables added one century later. The statue of Henry James was erected on the main lawn in the mid-twentieth. The present occupant . . ."

The trees protecting the manor were thick, and the country lane narrow. The crowd surged around the bus, hopeful: a wad of used chewing gum might fly out at any moment, or the thinly mustarded end of a hot dog. They watched the line of middle-aged ladies inside the bus—it was preferable to wait for a halt before trying to fit into the cramped lavatory. Mrs. Irving got there first as usual. A thin trickle of sanitized urine spread from under the bus. The crowd, barefooted, pressed closer.

The guide explained that the main lawn was the last example of old sod left in the country. He rocked on his feet, eyes closed—Sir Francis Drake had gone lawn bowling here; under that magnificent cedar (brought south by plane) Robert Bruce had formulated his Scottish policy; Spenser had dreamed from that window.

"You know," he went on as Mrs. Irving elbowed past him to her seat, "I have visited this place many times and its magic never ceases to haunt me. The present occupant, Jules Tanner, was born here. Now the history of the Tanners is an interesting one. They bought the place in the middle of the nineteenth century. . . ."

Mrs. Wrexham, implacable enemy of Mrs. Irving and leader of the group, edged down a window and stared out at the belt of birch trees and the high electric fence that sealed off Woodiscombe from the crowd.

On the other side of the road was the flat expanse of Salisbury Plain, covered with temporary buildings. A hand crept in through the small aperture and Mrs. Wrexham wound the window up again.

"I'm getting claustrophobia," announced Mr. Irving. "Can we go on now, please?"

Only the tallest turrets of Woodiscombe were visible, but the tourists were accustomed to this sort of thing. They had been taken to within three miles of the Tower of London and, parked in the bus parking lot, shown a film of beefeaters. A model of Buckingham Palace, with battery-operated toy soldiers changing the guard, was passed around from time to time. The crowd made real movement impossible.

The faces outside, some yellow, some pale brown, some white, were getting on Mrs. Irving's nerves. With an impatient twitch she lowered the imitation-leather blind over her window. From the crowd there came a hoarse, inexplicable laugh.

"When's the murder?" came a petulant voice. (It belonged to Mrs. Latham, representative of the American Women's Museum.) "I thought you said there was going to be a murder here!"

At a prearranged signal the electric bus started up, its whine scattering the crowd a few yards in front of the hood. Thin, scantily clad bodies climbed into the line of preserved elms on the Salisbury Plain side of the road. The bus edged forward.

"The murder is in preparation," said the guide with some coldness. "For those on the extended tour, that is. Woodiscombe will be revisited in three days time, when the murder has taken place."

"Woodiscombe revisited," sighed Mr. Irving, pretending in his gratitude at the movement of the bus that he could scarcely wait for the day.

"You're not on the extended tour," Mrs. Wrexham snapped.

"He has to do as Mrs. Irving says," remarked Mrs. Latham.

The crowd, disappointed once again, melted back onto the treeless uplands. The road was clear, and the bus moved between the trees smoothly.

Jules Tanner went from room to room, preparing his own murder. In the library, where the actual event would take place, he dusted the books and pulled out his old diaries, many written in multicolored inks and containing arcane clues to his death—others merely thoughts and beauty warnings of thirty years ago. "Rest the eyelashes," he read as he laid out the morocco-bound volumes on a table (how lovely his calligraphy had been then, as stern and frivolous as his pure profile and flowing hair). "After a complete rest, bathe in moonwater and reapply. To arch nostrils, lie in the dorsal position. When photographed, place tapering hands on cheeks as if supporting a Greek vase."

He paused, catching sight of himself in the long mirror between the windows, and sighed deeply. It was time he went, and the message from the State Department had not come a moment too soon—no, it was hardly believable that the man with faded, red-dyed locks, eyes that plummeted downward like fish trying desperately to get out of an aquarium, a nose that sprouted untintable gray hairs was the same as the Jules Tanner of the past.

"Your murder will take place on the first of May," went the cable delivered by the automatic mailman only two days ago. (And it was late April now, this Jules could see from the scurrying clouds, the frequent showers of refreshing rain.) "Woodiscombe Manor will then be listed as a Tourist Attraction, Grade One: The Setting of the Last Country House Murder. You are free to choose your murderer. Detective to be supplied by the State."

Yet, even after all these years of waiting, Jules felt a certain fear. For the last two days, before it had occurred to him to unearth the old journals and find there, as possible suspects, the people he had harmed most in the course of his selfish existence, he had wavered between the two most obvious choices: Bessy, who haunted him nightly with her threats of revenge, and old Cedric, who might well be dead now.

But did that really matter? It was impossible, bureaucracy having reached such a complicated stage, to get in touch with the Department and ask whether they intended to send their own assassin, if all the rigmarole of his choosing his own murderer was only for the history books. The murder was a piece of pure nostalgia, of course—strictly for the tourists. So what, if the most likely suspect had died many years ago? Or did an expired murderer make his own violent end a pale thing?

The journals yielded a rich crop of people once snubbed and despised by the Jules Tanner of those days—the beautiful, pre-Revolutionary Jules who had driven his own Hispano-Suiza into the dining room of the Ritz and sent mice running under the skirts of dancing debutantes. "Poor Lady Y was vomited over last night," proclaimed the naughty, spidery writing. "I douched her down with soda water, followed by a bottle of white wine." But who was Lady Y? And would she really bother, after all these years, to come down to Woodiscombe and kill him? Probably not—when to travel meant braving the crowd and obtaining a special permit for the opening of the Woodiscombe gates.

"Dear, plain Ursula proposed again last night," declared an entry in an ink once as bright green as the famous lawn. " 'Looks are not your basket,' I told her. 'Do you expect me to dress as the bride?' " Ursula, Ursula . . . now who . . . dead, probably, or otherwise living on in one of the rabbit warrens provided for the neo-rich . . . surrounded perhaps by ugly, non-breeding women like herself, enjoying an interminable middle age . . . only a menopausal madness would bring her to him, cause her to remember his insulting rejection. But the thought of it made Jules shudder. He moved from contemplation of his decay to the tall window that overlooked the garden—and smiled.

It had taken years of dedicated work to change the garden beyond recognition. The tourists of the future—three days in the future, when he would be dead, he realized, with that now familiar pang—would look in vain for the famous landmarks quoted by the guide. Paper flowers, each painted with the bright, leering features of a French sailor, scattered the noble lawn where once tennis had succeeded croquet, and croquet, lawn bowling. Shrubs of fiberglass—lovely, translucent plants that reflected the clouds on windy days and held raindrops like buds long after the passing of a shower—stood in symmetrical lines on the richly manured earth of the herbaceous borders. Plaster legs and feet climbed the facade of the house, blossoming into skirts of blue and pink silk at the onset of summer. On the gravel paths, rows of metal birds strutted and pecked, their motion set off by the faint incline of the land. (Once a week Jules collected them all and placed them at the top of the path again.)

It had been hard work, but the result was worth it. And now, looking out at the artificial garden, he saw there was much to be done before a suitable murderer could be selected. Spring showed in the faint blue of the shrubs. It was time to sprinkle glittering sand in the tropical garden and to plant the black, sticky lollipops among his painted flowers.

With a backward glance at the library—and for a moment he saw his body there; would they import a butler to discover him? he wondered—Jules Tanner strolled out into the open air.

2

The Appearance of Haines

Haines looked like the kind of Englishman Englishmen had rather liked before the Revolution. Then he would have been the typical middle-class commuter, a man with a suburban house and a face that somehow resembled that house—nose set set down like a prefabricated garage, at a convenient if unpleasing angle, eyes that looked out at the world like a couple of nylon-curtained windows. There was a streak of sarcasm in him perhaps, and this was reflected in a sardonic pull of the mouth which opened to show even, pointed teeth. He owned one ordinary suit, which hung in a small closet beside a spare pair of gardening pants and a worsted overcoat.

Now, of course, he was the sort of man whom everyone dreaded. He was the State snooper, with a license to carry arms. The hand, once bent around a clerk's pencil and a weekend lawn mower, now thumped on the door just when you expected it to and shot in, terrifyingly powerful in a leather glove, when you opened up. At the same time, many aspired to be like Haines. The work was varied when you reached Haines's rank, and the anonymity it took so many years to achieve meant you could assume several disguises. This was useful in what the Government had taken to calling times of trouble.

Of Haines's inner landscape we know little. He had so successfully erased the past that only tiny traces, like tartar on the teeth, remained of him. He had even given up humming, in case some ancient tune escaped by mistake. In the four walls of his dizzyingly high room he slept and woke and awaited orders with the precision of a slide rule. He spoke to no one in the hurtling elevators, and he walked with the squareness of his room around his narrow shoulders. Once he had cried out in his sleep, but the cry had gone unheard and was erased the next day from the bugging device behind the potted plant, Haines's only extravagance. He was the perfect detective, and felt no surprise when the command came.

The clothes arrived a few days later. They made an unusual clutter in the white room, and on the first night of their occupation they burst out of the closet all together. (To Haines's credit it must be said that no heartbeat was missed, the breathing on the machine continued steady and unbroken.) There was a Sherlock deerstalker and Inverness cape, in which Haines looked small and insignificant; a ridiculous Poirot suit with padded shoulders and accompanying moustaches; and a lace mobcap evoking Miss Marple.

Finally he chose Lord Peter Wimsey's outfit as being the most suitable for the occasion, but even as he donned it and turned dubiously in front of the mirror he wondered if the Department hadn't made some mistake.

Surely, even before the Revolution, gentlemen detectives hadn't had the nerve to go as far as this? The suit was of gray silk with mauve alpaca lapels, and a real diamond pin gleamed coyly from the recesses of a light-gray necktie. White spats struck a bizarre note in the room, which seemed to shrink back from the useless things with their little jet buttons and their way of appearing to vanish up Haines's legs like a rabbit going back into a hat. A cloud-gray silk hat completed the picture—and this Haines clutched nervously as if it might explode at any moment. It was the first time in his long career that he had felt uneasy in a costume.

However, there was work to be done. Eyes were carefully averted from him in the elevator, though speculation mounted once he had climbed into the freshly supplied Buick and driven off. This was something on a grand scale—and the radio confirmed it later in the day when the "secret" was given out. To boost the economy, a great country house murder was under way. Advance bookings from tourists the world over had meant the construction of new hotels, and jobs for the unemployed.

What made this such an extraordinary occasion, of course, was Woodiscombe's uniqueness: the last country house, and the last country house occupant. The public was well acquainted with the existence of the victim, Jules Tanner, for he was often quoted as the only surviving example of the decadent pre-Revolutionary days. Many envied Haines as he drove carefully through the crowded streets to Wiltshire.

3

The Quarters of the Rich

Pure coincidence—or, as his detractors claimed later when Haines was to be blamed for everything that had gone wrong in the country, collaborationist tendencies—led the prim but gaudily attired detective to bump straight into the chief suspect on the first stage of his journey south. It happened as follows: Haines, despite his vanished memory and his soft-voiced contempt for the English way of life of the past, would once or twice a year take advantage of his special card and visit the area where the once-rich had been permitted to spin out the residue of their useless lives.

He wasn't alone in indulging this form of mild curiosity. The crowd was kept out by means of an invisible barrier, the streets were free of public transport, and there were gardens—populated, it was true, by other distinguished visitors to the zone, but gardens nonetheless; and charges of nostalgia were seldom brought against officials of Haines's rank even if they went there fairly regularly. Haines, as we know, was a cautious man, and he kept his excursions down to a minimum. On this occasion, perhaps, he wasn't fully aware of the strange spectacle he presented, but it was against his better judgment that he flashed his card at the uniformed guide at the barrier and eased the Buick down the shabby streets of the quarter.

It was a fine day, punctuated by bursts of stinging rain that fell greedily onto the flowered hats of their wearers, as if determined to wash away the last traces of privilege and power. Haines strolled in the gardens, his little bugging device (concealed behind the diamond tiepin) bringing him snatches of the old type of conversation.

"No, it was after that that she went off with Sandy, after Joel had been made Ambassador to Beirut or somewhere and they sold the Boltons' house," insisted one voice. "Don't you remember, she got a hundred thousand for it and when Mikey came back from Athens with that terrible boy there was nowhere for him to stay?"

"You've got the wrong woman altogether," another voice—a man's—came in querulously. "Think of Dora, Dora Carstairs, I mean, the one who married the maharaja and then that football player and then what's-his-name—that's the one you're thinking of. She never had anything to do with Sandy at all."

Haines, with a pretended cough, fiddled at his throat and lowered the volume of the minitransistor. His expressionless face under the gray silk hat was attracting some attention, and he glanced quickly up at the mock-Georgian facades of the living quarters as if visiting the area for the first time.

"Sandy always hated Dora," the voice went on, tired by now. "In fact, Sandy was queer from the start. No question about that."

"You're thinking of Mikey," barked the first voice—a ginny woman's voice that caused Haines to look around for the refreshment stand where these people played at being drinkers and barmen. Yes—there it was, all gay red-and-white stripes, with a handful of men dressed like himself popping fizzy tablets into water-filled champagne glasses. He sauntered over to take a closer look at the mock paddock behind the tent, where two old horses nibbled at the worn grass.

The voices grew louder as he approached, and Haines, only half listening to them, came suddenly to a halt.

"That's why I'm so simply petrified about poor Jules's murder," the woman's voice was saying. "Because absolutely everyone confuses Violet with Dora and so they'll think I'm mixed up in it."

"What do you mean?"

The speakers could be identified by now, as the only

two people engaged in active conversation at the entrance to the tent (the others, mostly men in their early eighties, brought a faint hum of old racing talk to Haines's ears, but he was trained to cut out interference), and of the two Haines instantly recognized the woman.

There had been a scandal some years back when it was discovered that the make-believe black market (without which the once-wealthy would have gone unaware of their perilous position in society) had in fact been infiltrated by earnest operators from the outside. Steaks, eggplant, and asparagus—the real thing, not the skillfully disguised vitamin-and-protein product—had appeared mysteriously in the zone. For a week or two, photographs of the inside ringleader—this woman, there was no doubt about that—had covered the front pages of the newspapers. She had gone unpunished, and no reasons had been given.

"But you're not Dora," snapped the man, who looked, as Haines wandered innocently nearer, on the point of extinction. He was rocking gently on his feet and puffing at a grass cigar, and his old eyes gazed with tired panic from either side of an unscalable nose. "If you'd ever had anything to do with Sandy, and you were Dora, and Dora had been caught with Sandy, which thank God she wasn't, then—" The cigar went out and the man threw it impatiently on the ground. "And you're not Violet either," he concluded triumphantly.

"Do you want us to be late for bridge?" the woman cried. For the first time she took in the presence of Haines a few feet off and drew herself up in suspicion. "Are you making a fourth?" she demanded of him.

Haines gave a low bow which he recognized too late as coming from his days rehearsing Poirot (before the clothes arrived). Just in time he stopped himself from answering in the Gallic accent it had been so difficult to learn, straightened up and nodded mutely.

"Who are you then?"

The owner of the man's voice was pointing excitedly at the bridge tables set up under the trees beyond the paddock. "A rubber before the next shower, Dora! Do you remember when there used to be room to play indoors? Why, I can remember whole rooms set aside for bridge. Do you remember, Dora, when there were rooms for billiards too?" His voice trailed away, and water streamed from his eyes onto high, weathered cheekbones.

"I'm not Dora," the woman said briskly. "You know very well who I am." She lowered her voice—pointlessly, as it happened, for Haines's device could pick up anything—"I'm Bessy, and that's why I'm so afraid that some ridiculous detective will mix up Violet with Dora like everyone does and Violet will go and tell him I was married to Jules or something."

Stealthily (Haines was good at stealth and apparent unconcern) the small man in the gray silk suit with mauve lapels turned away from the speakers and strolled to the edge of the paddock. One of the horses was lying down, the other trembling as an old man dressed as a jockey tried to clamber on its back.

"You're Bessy!" The fretful voice drifted up to him from under the gray tie. "You were Bessy Pontoon and then you married that Italian and then you went off with that queer Jules Something-or-other. I remember perfectly well, of course I do."

"I never even met Jules Tanner," the woman's voice hissed. "That's the mistake Violet always makes. For God's sake, Fred, anyone could be listening now—they're trying to find Jules's murderer." She snatched at the old man's arm and led him past where Haines was standing. They made for the bridge tables, where an ironic cheer went up. A steady rain began to fall.

"Anyway, Jules wasn't queer," said Bessy's voice, deep in Haines's chest when she thought herself well out of earshot. "What an old-fashioned word to use."

"You should never have had anything to do with him or Sandy, Dora," came the faint rejoinder.

Haines climbed thoughtfully into the Buick and dictated some possible clues before driving off.

4

Father and Son

Jules's father was sitting in what had once been the morning room (Jules had cleared all the rooms of their famous contents and had stored the beautiful carpet, the Van Dyck portraits, and the rare porcelain in an old storage shed outside) and was reading a yellowed newspaper that proclaimed from its front page the arrest of some suffragettes and the murder of some grand duke or other at Sarajevo. From time to time he lifted a cup and rested his drooping moustaches carefully on the little china moustache-catcher before sipping at the contents.

Jules could tell it really was his father and not some well-primed agent of the State by the fact that all Sir Clovis's favorite knickknacks had sprouted mysteriously around him—the egg timer with the red-and-black sands of Africa running through the waist when the egg was four minutes, the round silver hot plate where Sir Clovis kept his muffins, and a host of other details which only a member of the family would recognize.

A fine oak table, long ago left by Jules to rot in the cellar, supported all these treasures—and the tweedy elbow of Sir Clovis, who was picking his teeth behind the newspaper, rested on it firmly. Jules sat down opposite him and helped himself to an Indian dish of rice and fish.

"You're late again," came the muffled voice of the patriarch. "I hear you're to be murdered shortly, too. Surely you have a good deal of correspondence to catch up with?"

The paper was lowered a fraction as a ghostly, uniformed maid glided in with fresh coffee and departed again. Jules, twisting in the massive chair, felt pouring into his system all the remorse and anguish of his childhood and youth, all the hatred of his later years. How often, before the sudden disappearance of Sir Clovis on a hunting expedition in South Africa, had he sat like this, toying with his country house breakfast and swearing in unheard words so violent that his father would shift sometimes uneasily in his seat and remark on the inclemency of the weather. How often had he planned, with that blunt fish knife engraved with docile trout and spiky silver weeds on the fluted handle, to kill him there and then, put an end to the whole business!

Oddly, by the time the excellent sirloin reached the table, and a suitable knife to go with it, honed by old Bills on the sharpening stone outside the servants' hall, Jules's fantasy had usually faded. In the end he came to accept the morning agony as some fault in his digestive system. Reverting effortlessly to the early years of guilt, Jules considered his father's charges and saw them to be true.

One letter he had been trying to send for over a quarter of a century now, yet—however many times he reminded himself at night that the lovely scented envelope must go off to its destination in the morning—when morning came it always remained on the first stage of the journey, the windowsill in his bedroom.

Sometimes he blamed progress—the village mailman, who had taken the trouble to climb up to Jules's room and stand over him, suggesting possible ways of ending his letters, had been succeeded by an angry yellow van that stood, siren blaring, at the gates of Woodiscombe for only sixty seconds. There was no driver in the van—or no visible driver, anyway—and the crowd was liable to snatch at the mail as it was handed over. And then all the addresses had changed. Jules found himself unable to fathom the codes and numbers, a simple address like 17 Rossetti Gardens,

Chelsea, having been replaced by WO2tnxcyL. He regretted nevertheless the particular unmailed missive, which came to mind at his father's unfortunate mention of the subject—a proposal of marriage to a once-famous film star that, if it had arrived with the rest of the fan mail, would most certainly have changed the course of his life.

"Dear Gloria," said the serpentine brown writing on crinkly blue paper, "I can offer you the most lovely of homes, the truest of hearts. How can I describe the haven I have here for you, the doves cooing in the eaves, the soft splash of water as it runs under Japanese bridges? Come here; be mine."

The name on the envelope had changed many times since the installation at Woodiscombe of TV—Marilyn, Natalie, Ali, Tuesday—but the address, Sunset Boulevard, was always the same. It was impossible to know how to signify this in code. Jules's eyes filled with tears as he thought of the forgotten letter, and his heart jumped in filial rage.

"Your mother tells me you never sent a Christmas card to Nanny," continued Sir Clovis. "Your tax affairs are in a shocking state. How many days are left to you?"

So Sir Clovis would be with him until the hour of his death! Jules gritted his teeth and rose from the table, striding to the morning-room window and looking out at just what he had expected to see—the old devil had reinstated the rosebeds and the sunken garden with its symmetrical arrangement of Elizabethan herbs; the "white garden" where his mother had posed for a painting was in full, sickening bloom.

"I don't much care for your changes," Sir Clovis remarked, following his son's horrified gaze. "Do you think the tourists are going to put up with a lot of cheap paper plants? And glass shrubs collect dust."

Jules felt the impotence of childhood fill what he now realized was a smaller, almost prep-school frame. He reached out a hand, and a golden silk tassel from an invisible curtain swung obediently into his palm. He fidgeted with it, as he had done through all the years of his adolescence.

"Don't fidget with that thing!" Sir Clovis, stomach satisfied, left the breakfast table and walked over ponderously to join his son. An arm descended on Jules's shoulder. With terror Jules stared at the tiny, living forest of gray hairs on Sir Clovis's knuckles, and smelled the aftermath of complacently munched toast and pipe tobacco.

Oh, yes, this was his father all right! No skillful disguise this, to cloud over his last precious days on earth. Sir Clovis's voice came softer now, with that faint sibilance caused by a chipped front tooth (a too-close encounter with a leopard on safari). He cleared his throat with a Delphic rumble.

"My dear Jules." (What could this sudden tone of

friendship mean? Jules trembled and threw the silken tassel against the windowpane.) A thick brocade curtain fell around them both, and Sir Clovis pushed it back, glancing up with pleasure at the heavy curtain.

"My dear son, I have but one thing to ask of you. Your end and the end of Woodiscombe are at hand. I simply demand . . . "

Jules shook his head, burst from his father's embrace and stood facing him, defiant at last. The breakfast table vanished, leaving an assortment of Sir Clovis's knickknacks hanging suspended in midair.

" . . . that I should be the one to commit the murder," finished Sir Clovis as his face grew transparent and the moustache, taken unawares by the imminent disappearance of its owner, lingered like an undusted cobweb by the curtainless windows. "Who else?" whispered the fading specter of Sir Clovis. His feet, in painfully shining brown shoes, were the last to go. The egg timer whisked out of the room suddenly, as if manipulated by wires.

"Who else?" moaned Jules, surveying the empty room. With effort he retraced his steps to the library and pulled out the journals.

5

The Journey South

Haines drew nearer. The Buick was the only car on the crowded highway running on gas, and there were curious glances from the cramped occupants of the electric trucks and airport buses as it roared noisily along, leaving a trail of strange-smelling fog in its wake. From the pedestrian bridges above the highway (built over with houses now, which gave a peculiar Venice-like effect, as if the road were in fact a giant river and the trucks small craft of various descriptions) the crowd stared down at the flamboyant detective and let out a halfhearted cheer. Despite the enthusiastic voices on the radio, it seemed unlikely that the last country house murder, and the revenue it would bring in, were the solution to their problems. The arrival of more tourists made existing conditions even worse, and a decision on whether to hang the eventual murderer had not yet been reached. Nevertheless, Haines was an arresting sight—and they cheered.

A miniature computer had been built into the dashboard of the car, and Haines fed it with the information he had picked up in central London. "A woman named Bessy referred to a certain Dora and a certain Violet, both former people," he addressed the walnut control panel. "Who is Bessy, reference black market crime, and who are Dora and Violet? Further, a man named Fred, appearance neocolonial, neo-capitalist: background and past crimes required. Possibly irrelevant, two men named Sandy and Mikey. Grade One: confirm or refute charges of Jules Tanner's homosexuality."

Haines sat back while the machine went to work. A warm afternoon had brought thick bunches of picnickers to the shoulders of the highway and for a moment the faintest trace of a memory stirred in the white desert of his mind. His mother . . . a hamper containing sandwiches with real bread and delicious green cucumber . . . a bicycle he had just been given for his birthday. Haines allowed a faint smile to flicker at the edge of his mouth, then drew his lips together quickly. He had no intention of walking in at the scene of the crime with the remnants of nostalgia all over his face.

It might have seemed odd to him, had he remembered his school days, how wrong the Orwells and Huxleys had been about the society of the future. No Big Brother was needed for those in power to be able to pick out a nonconformist, no watchful screen to report on deviant activities. It was impossible to move, in such crowded conditions, without a hundred people knowing exactly what you were doing, foolish to indulge in thoughts of the past when there was no healing solitude to remove the uneasy expression such feelings engendered. The Government hadn't even needed to develop telepathic methods; a guilty man in a crowd was always visible.

Now the computer was disgorging ribbons bearing the answers to Haines's questions. He fed them into a cassette player and slowed a little, keeping the Buick to the middle lane although by doing this he was probably holding up the faster electric traffic considerably. He was a tourist attraction today, and he enjoyed the inconvenience this caused—at least he was going faster than the old buses, laden with Japanese, which clung to the shoulder of the road and disturbed the picnickers as they rumbled past.

"Bessy Pontoon is the woman," said the silvery voice from the cassette transcribing machine. "Daughter of the Eleventh Earl of Farc, no other offspring surviving. Married first John Marker, better known as pop idol Crax, then for the second time the American novelist Paul Couples, also resulting in divorce. Two records of her friendship with the victim Jules Tanner are in existence."

The four-inch-square screen on the dashboard flashed a twenties photograph of a young woman with shingled hair standing beside what appeared to be another young woman with loose, flowing hair. Haines looked contemplative.

"Deduction One," he dictated as a blurred snap of the pair at a cross-country horse race grew on the screen. "Before the so-called sexual revolution of the sixties the victim wore long hair."

"Dora and Violet are Siamese twins," continued the even voice. "A successful operation to separate them was performed when they were twenty, but they preferred to be together and have since remained tied to each other by means of a scarf or other artificial methods. Rumors of their involvement with the victim have not yet been verified."

Haines sighed. Not for the first time he felt certain misgivings about the assignment. It was both difficult and distasteful to have to work out the relationships between the once-rich.

"Fred is one of ours," the voice went on. "Identification secret; age forty; in permanent disguise in the quarter as a retired colonel in his seventies. Your visit this morning has already been reported. You are required to visit headquarters in Woodisford before proceeding to the manor."

Later, Haines was to remember the chill of premonition he had felt at this, the sudden guilt—an emotion he had never before experienced—bring the first-ever blush to his pale cheeks. He drove on apparently unperturbed, his mind racing. True, he hadn't informed the Department of his intention to visit the quarter before setting out, but that had been because he had no idea, until he climbed into the Buick, of his desire to go there. And after all, he had found the most likely suspect almost at once . . . did they wish, simply to congratulate him before his work began? This, Haines had to admit, was improbable. Congratulations were unheard of in the Department.

Woodisford headquarters, a former vicarage, was protected by high steel walls from the crowded roads of West Wiltshire. The Buick was allowed through after careful scrutiny of its occupant, and went slowly and cautiously along the neglected drive leading to the house. About fifty yards short of its destination a hissing sound puzzled Haines and the car sloped sideways, coming to a halt against a boulder. Sweating a little, Haines clambered out to review the situation.

"A flat tire!" he said aloud, his surprise at the memories it brought to him (combined with the first experience of guilt they made an unpalatable mixture) causing him to lose his calm. "Well, imagine that, a flat tire," he added inanely.

A squat man in a heavy overcoat materialized from somewhere behind the house and strolled down to stand by the side of the Buick.

"You seem somewhat flustered, Mr. Haines," he remarked, in the punctilious tones of the New Accent, which marked him instantly as a Government official. Most members of the crowd had been too lazy and ignorant to relearn how to speak.

Haines started back, feeling the guilt make little pinpricks of high color on his face. Against the khaki background of the official's coat, he saw his father kneel by the side of the road to change a tire and heard him curse the new Government and all its doings. "Old Army tires," Haines's father grumbled. "The country's gone to wrack and ruin."

"Come this way," said the careful, flat voice. "The car will be repaired during your stay at Woodiscombe. If you need it, that is," he went on, leading Haines into the old vicarage. "This way, please."

"If I need it?"

More memories flooded the vulnerable vacuum of his mind, this time of the school where Haines had sat in a silent row of bare-kneed boys, waiting for the leather strap to sting the extended palms of the hands of his friends—the friends he had just five minutes before betrayed to the teacher. It had been then and there that he had decided to remain all his life firmly on the side of authority. With the friendly, direct gaze of the sneak, Haines trotted after the official into an expensively furnished room.

"Depending on your success at Woodiscombe, of course."

Digesting this, Haines took the upright chair offered him. A faint strain in the atmosphere, a tightening of the air in the already stuffy office suggested they were waiting for the arrival of a more important person. He pondered the possible complications of the case. Was this Bessy Pontoon an unacceptable murderer? Were they, perhaps, about to inform him that he must do the actual killing himself? Haines cringed a little at the thought. He had brought about the end of many undesirable people, but he had never actually murdered someone with his own hands. A blunt instrument hung for a moment in the air before him, its thick spiked end liberally smeared with blood and hair. He repressed a shudder.

The important official entered the room to a general exhalation of breath, and the atmosphere became immediately both lighter and sharper, like at the onset of a thunderstorm. He went to sit behind the desk as if there were no other possible place for him, straddling the mock-Chippendale chair and staring with disconcerting amazement at his visitor.

Haines was used to this sort of thing and immediately

offered his name. There was no point in playing around with officials, waiting for them to speak first because they had summoned you and so on. They liked to pretend, Haines knew, to a total ignorance of the situation—to need a reminder of why you were there at all and why they must put up with it.

"In connection with the Woodiscombe murder," the second official corroborated in a doleful voice.

"Ah, yes." The important official quickly doodled on a pad. (This was intended to terrify, too, but Haines was used to it. He had learned many years ago the trick of reading the words that grew under officials' hands as they sat at their desks. He nodded.

"You visited the Quarter in London. Now you must realize, Mr.—er—Haines, that our overseas visitors will be very disappointed if the murder is solved too quickly. Bessy Pontoon, we agree, is an acceptable suspect. However . . . "

An old-fashioned rose sprouted on the pad. The official noticed it and crossed it out with impatience. He leaned back in his chair, fixing Haines with a stare.

"A life of Jules Tanner's sort is bound to produce many suspects. Don't you agree?"

Haines assented meekly. A question bubbled to his lips and stayed there, detectable only by little beads of spit on the cracked skin.

"It's interesting that you chose the Lord Peter Wimsey outfit," the official went on in a pleasant, almost chatty tone. "Any particular reason?"

The question forced its way out of Haines's mouth before he had time to extinguish it.

"Will the murderer be executed?" he said. "I mean—"

The official exchanged a glance with his underling and then permitted a short, breezy laugh to come from both of them. This was immediately succeeded by a frown and furious scribbling on the pad. Haines's heart thumped, and the sound returned to him magnified by the bug under his tiepin. Silently he cursed himself.

"That information has not yet been given out." The official rose from his chair and held out his hand. "We simply wished to remind you," he said mildly, as if the visit had been a social call, a simple formality requested by Haines himself, "that there are certain dangerous elements in society." He accompanied Haines to the door, a chummy hand on his shoulder. "For instance"—he seemed almost abstracted by now, gazing down the hall with the air of a kind, busy man—"for instance, there are people who would like to see the end of you and me, Haines. Has that ever occurred to you? Forget it, anyway, forget it." The hand propelled Haines onto the steps of the vicarage and the second official mumbled something about the punctured tire.

"Never mind that!" The important official gave another of his mysterious laughs. "Go along there on foot, Mr. Haines. You may see what I mean."

"On foot?"

Haines glanced down at his spats, which were marching ahead of him down the steps and onto the untidy gravel. "But—"

Then he saw the electric truck—one of the green ones with red lettering on the outside, which meant a very high-up person indeed. A second later he realized the important official must have come all the way from London in it. A faint drumming from his mini-transistor filled his ears.

"Good luck!"

The voice of the important official followed him down the drive to the gate.

6

Jules's Dream of the East

Jules went to lie down in the midnight-blue room, where his aged Vietnamese manservant was waiting with the opium pipes and wooden-block pillow and had drawn the thick velvet curtains embroidered with stars. For a time there was silence between them as Jules puffed and old Sing fiddled on the floor with the equipment. Then Jules, propping himself on an elbow, began to speak.

"I wish Cedric would come to me, Sing. I've left all the doors and windows open and there are letters from him scattered about the house. I think, Sing, that jealousy is the best motive for murder. Cedric was so jealous of me, you know, in the days when I was in the theater. It was a mere matter of looks—but Sing, how important they are! Cedric had such ideas for himself, such fancies, yet he was forever cast as Horatio, as Macduff, as the husband in *Hedda Gabler*, the schoolteacher in *The Three Sisters*—it was so tragic for him!"

"Mr. Tanner had the heroic roles," murmured Sing. Smoke from the pipes filled the room and Jules sighed happily, his eyes fixed on the only piece of furniture he had allowed to remain there—a chest of drawers with the second drawer pulled out. A family of young cats was playing in it.

"Cedric took up singing as a last resort." Jules chuckled. "Upstairs there is a letter from him bemoaning the fact that he was to play the part of Seneca in that Italian play . . . when he had so longed for Nero! How many times was poor Cedric cuckolded, abandoned, or even forgotten at the end of the play? We cannot count, can we, Sing? When kitchen-sink drama came, poor Cedric thought his turn had come at last, yet it was I who turned down the part of Jimmy Porter. And the Noel Coward revival—"

"You were brilliant in that," chanted Sing. "It was only a pity that Mr. Tanner gave his performances here and without an audience. Many have said that."

"And they were right!" Jules's sleepy, malicious voice grew softer and his eyes closed. A tawny kitten scuttled toward his prone figure through the smoke and Sing quietly shooed it away.

"His first and last great heroic part." Jules's voice

came haltingly now. "To murder me! For a world audience. Yes, Sing, he must come."

For a while there was silence in the room, then Sing crept away, leaving his master alone. Jules, waiting for Cedric, turned in his sleep and groaned. For instead of Cedric . . .

Rain was falling in the streets of Zenane, southern Laos. French colonial houses, each with its heavily pruned, white-painted tree, stood by the banks of the Mekong. Bougainvillaea climbed over facades intended to support wisteria; fungus grew in the interstices of the brittle gold chairs imported from Paris. On the upper floor of one of these houses, with its mournful view of the brown river and its framed prints of French towns, were David and the other English doctors. They sipped at mugs of instant coffee and discussed the new hospital—no more than a long hut, really—which repeated appeals to charity in the home country had finally managed to produce. David was complaining: that supplies took weeks to come down from Vientiane, that the war would wipe out the few patients they managed to cure, that he had run out of money and saw no way of getting home. His face, so sharply outlined before Jules's eyes now, was long and bony with large black eyes that seemed, because of the bruises of tiredness under them, to be melting and spreading over his cheeks. His shoulders were thin and hunched.

"Tell me about it all!" Jules, conscious of his visitor

status, sat plumply forward on the gold chair as if expecting to make conversation in a drawing room. He was pleased with himself; it had been difficult getting permission to come to the south, to the border of Thailand. He had sketched the Mekong all morning, filling in the colorful figures of the Lao and the slender canoes as they drifted past. The best of his looks had gone, but he still cut a fine figure in the tropical suits made to measure in London before his departure on the world tour.

"Come to the hospital," David said. The other doctors, suspicious of Jules, were leafing through medical journals and talking among themselves. There was a dance tonight. The Lao were very proud at having organized it. A mention of the local rice wine brought a burst of rueful laughter from the group.

Jules, shrinking from the sight of the pregnant woman on the narrow bed, her bundle from the village lying firmly on her feet, followed the young English doctor down the ward. A couple of men groaned with pain and Jules quickened his steps.

"How very . . . dedicated you are! I mean, what brought you out here?" He was conscious of his fat, smooth face, and patted it anxiously. They were standing outside the hospital now, with the jungle only a few feet away. The crumbling roofs of Zenane were invisible through the trees.

"This godforsaken place?" David smiled. "I suppose

you'll say you met a character straight out of fiction when you get home. Idealism is probably the answer. Now I'm stuck here and my ideals have gone. How about that?"

"My dear, don't be so self-conscious," Jules cried. "Act out your part properly. Take to drink or something!"

David gave a bitter laugh, while Jules stared at him intently and an outsize blue butterfly skimmed past them, heading for the jungle's inner lake. Jules felt the excitement of money, power, and ownership.

"Maybe I can help you," he said.

"Well . . . could you?" David seized Jules's arm and Jules made himself feel an electric shock run up it. "I'm desperate . . . I gambled my money away in Vientiane when I last went up there on leave . . . it's a question of the fare. Nothing more."

The two men strolled back into town along the monsoon-washed track. Under heavy skies a little market had been set up, selling raffia suitcases. Jules stopped and bought one, dangling it like a handbag against his thigh. "Well, why not?" he said lightly, "We'll see."

The party turned out to be a Chinese funeral, held in the ruined temples on the fringes of the jungle. A white bamboo coffin smoked quietly on its base, attached by strings for the spirit to travel along to various spots on the ground and the roof of the temple. The crowd—Cambodian, Lao, and Thai—lighted fires among the bushes and plunged fists into wooden rice pots. The other English doctors drank their own supply of whisky and sang Scottish songs.

Afterward, Jules and David lay on Jules's bed in Zenane's only hotel. Jules slept deeply, half aware from time to time of the rustlings of small animals beyond the mosquito net that engulfed them both like an enormous wedding dress. At some point David must have crept away, for Jules awakened alone, smiling. His arm reached out across the sheet, which was damp already from the morning air.

"Sing! Sing!"

Jules struggled to sitting position, flinging the wooden block on which his head had rested across the floor of the darkened room. Sing's footsteps sounded outside and the door opened, letting in a shaft of light.

"Mr. Tanner has not found Cedric?"

Sing knelt on the floor, gathering the pipes into the raffia case Jules had bought in Zenane. Jules wept, pointing for the curtains to be drawn back. Early evening sun poured into the room and the cats leaped back into their drawer.

"Sing, I saw David again!" cried Jules. "Surely . . . surely he wouldn't come?"

"It's a long way," Sing said.

"Yes, but, Sing, he stole all that money from me. And then disappeared. And then—"

"You found the doctor in England and he went to prison," Sing said smiling. "He will not come to kill Mr. Tanner."

"Did he marry, Sing? Is that why he wanted the money to get home?" Jules paced the room, his hand to his head. "I'm so confused, Sing—I wasn't so ugly then, would you say?"

The door was pushed wider open and a woman came in. Neither Jules nor Sing saw her at first.

"It was all a long time ago," Sing reminded his master.

7

Haines Arrives

It was many years since Haines had gone anywhere on foot. He had forgotten, as a result of his car-borne existence (whisked from the subterranean cavern under his apartment block to the depths of Government office buildings), what his height was in relation to other people, whether he was thin, ordinary or plump. The first shock he received on reaching the country lane leading to Woodiscombe was how small the crowd had become, how puny compared with his own private estimation of himself as a short man with pleasingly slender extremities. Elbows as brittle and pointed as old men's fingers jostled his stomach as he made his way carefully along the uplands side of the road. Heads no bigger than coconuts bobbed at the level of his necktie, causing an almost deafening hubbub to rise from the concealed transistor. The feet of the crowd were tiny, and they were identically shod in rough straw slippers, so that the effect was that of a giant millipede, surging in all directions at once and breaking into several pieces at the advent of a tourist bus, then joining together again smoothly when it had passed.

Haines, towering above the mob, made a surprising-enough spectacle in his gray silk suit to cause a vacuum—only a few inches, it was true, but a breathing space—around his person. He carried his chin high, pretending not to notice the cries of laughter and amazement at his appearance. A tinny rattle from the crowd indicated that nearly everyone had a transistor. So it was likely that he had been quickly identified as the detective involved in the last country house murder case. Otherwise, he reflected grimly, he would probably have been torn to pieces by now.

For Haines had hardly expected so violent and mobile a crowd. He wondered if this was the reason for the important official's suggestion that he continue his journey on foot—an oblique way of showing him the state of near-anarchy in the provinces? Or a reminder that, if he disappointed the overseas visitors with a banal solution to the murder, his lot would be no better than the crowd's?

The sight of tattered shirts and jeans, so fashionable among the rich before the Revolution, filled him with revulsion, and he glanced down protectively at the outrageous costume he already considered his own badge of identity. It was unthinkable that this case had been handed to him as some kind of test, that the Department was in fact displeased with him and had decided to try him out one last time before either retaining or disposing of him. . . . Yet the idea, so horrible when it had first come to him at Woodisford headquarters, that he might be told suddenly in the next couple of days of his own role as murderer, returned with force as, stomach turning from the smell of the crowd, he pushed his way through it to the manor.

"Of course not," he muttered, held up for a moment by the surging masses. What could be more banal, more bourgeois, pre-Revolutionary theater than that? The detective as murderer—of course not! But the Department, although he was afraid even to admit it secretly, was sometimes short on imagination. Haines detached himself from what transpired to be a line for food at a makeshift wooden stall by the side of the road, and pressed forward more quickly. He was beginning to see his dilemma with clarity now. In case—just in case—he was picked for the role at the last moment (for political reasons of some kind: to teach the crowd once again not to hanker for a decadent life, perhaps) he must find a murderer with speed and broadcast the name to the waiting tourists. But he had been told to make the case as complicated as possible, to outdo all the great plots of the past—and how could he do this at speed?

Haines frowned, forcing himself to relax by bringing to mind a jumbo crossword puzzle, as he always did when threatened with anxiety. First he made up the clues, then filled in Across before concentrating on Down. "Man most suitable as exterminator of stately home occupant laughs before a Spanish maiden," he mumbled. "Ha-ines," he concluded miserably. "Polite domestic best shows the world how to commit crime." With a sinking heart Haines filled in Civil Servant, the Servant running down from the S of the Haines, and trudged on.

"Excuse me, please."

Four or five arms from the crowd formed a barrier across Haines's path and he came to a standstill, staring down for the first time at the thin, worried faces below his splendid tiepin.

"Have you a food voucher, please?" said what seemed to be several voices at once.

"A food voucher?" Haines tried to shake off the clinging arms. "No, do I need one?" he added haughtily. "I am on my way to the manor, as a matter of fact."

The arms dropped, but a roar from the crowd went up as they did so. Haines saw, in one of the rapid summings-up for which he had received promotion in his job, that the situation was perilous. He remained, as he had taught himself in the past, absolutely still in the face of danger and looked expressionlessly down at the crowd.

"Throw away your vouchers!" The mob on the uplands was pouring through the line of preserved trees onto the road, making a crowd so dense that Haines was lifted off his feet slightly, his balance going as he pitched forward onto greasy heads and bony shoulder blades which poked through torn shirts.

From this greater height he could see the temporary buildings on the uplands, the ramshackle wooden sky-scrapers and abandoned, rusting farm machinery. Some of the crowd had stayed behind there, for what looked like rows of white cabbages on a small area of plowed earth could just be identified as the overalled behinds of women sowing seed. Tiny creatures—children, probably—danced around a big bonfire on the horizon. The ancient burial mounds on the road to Stonehenge supported lookout towers made of cut preserved larches and roofed with yew. Haines swore to himself, promising that he would report this vandalism to the Government.

"Down with the Government!" the crowd shouted, unanimous now they had been joined by the others. "Set fire to your vouchers!"

Haines was forgotten as he lurched horizontally over the heads of the crowd and past a half-trampled booth which bore the legend "Supplementary Benefit Holders Only" to the gates of Woodiscombe Manor. With a desperate movement he punched at the electric bell on the gate before being carried back again several feet, like a victorious football player, on the shoulders of the angry crowd. The next wave brought him right up against the gate and an electric shock ran viciously through his system. The gate opened a crack, and he was thrown in. Trembling, still clutching his wrecked topper, Haines walked uncertainly toward the house.

By the time he reached the door the roar of the crowd was distant and muffled. Somewhere in the garden a peacock gave a hoarse scream. Haines started nervously and banged the brass knocker with unaccustomed force.

8

Preparing the Body

Jules was lying in a hammock in the garden, talking to Bessy. He had been horrified at first, after his unpleasant encounter with David and the strain of Sir Clovis's visit, to find her standing waiting for him in the blue room, but he was relieved now to have someone to talk to other than the obsequious Sing. Sing had brought them tea, and Bessy was stretched out on an Aubusson carpet among the glass shrubs. A flock of metal flamingos, their vermilion wings catching the last of the sun's rays, strutted delicately around them.

"I agree Cedric is the obvious choice," Bessy was saying. (Jules, in spite of himself, admired her peach silk dress and Veronica Lake hair, which fell provocatively over her eyes.) "But, Jules, don't you remember our times together? Aren't I—alas—the suspect they're all waiting for?"

With the coquettish air of a fading actress, Bessy tossed the long strand of hair out of her left eye and smiled directly at Jules. A brooch in the shape of an amethyst-and-sapphire cocktail bar glinted on her now revealed shoulder, and as she moved, miniature diamond martinis shook in a transparent moonstone shaker. Her famous Dorothy Lamour smile lingered on her face after Jules had turned away impatiently.

"If only, Jules, you hadn't upset me so much and I hadn't made such a fuss about it at the time. All they have to do, you know, is look up the old newspaper clippings—"

Jules groaned and closed his eyes. A cloud had passed over the sun, and the crowd seemed to be roaring louder than usual, so that he was transported immediately to the Orient Express, his engagement trip with Bessy, to the darkened sleeper and the rushing wheels that were carrying them, after a disgruntled visit to Venice, to Constantinople and beyond. Bessy had climbed into his sleeper and was stroking his golden hair with her fingernails. Chanel No. 5 floated up to his nostrils through the soot-and-garlic smell of the train. Jules edged away, reaching for his pack of cigarettes with a pretendedly casual hand.

"Jules, it must be now! Jules, I want you so much!" He had never heard Bessy sound like this before and he tried to laugh it off, sitting bolt upright on the narrow couch and pulling his silk dressing gown close to his body. But she meant it. There were tears, screams, the pulling of the emergency cord . . .

"It is dangerous to lean out of the window," Jules murmured, translating the sign across from him. He opened his eyes. Bessy was still there on the carpet at his feet, a half-rueful smile on her face.

"Women never forgive that," she said softly. "I'm not quite sure I've forgiven it yet, Jules darling. I had no idea, you see."

"You took your revenge," Jules pointed out.

"Oh, yes! But my life is so miserable now. I'd rather die for having murdered you than live on with all those stupid old men in a sort of open prison. I can't tell you what it's like, Jules. Racing all day, and bridge when it's raining, only you have to play in the rain, if you see what I mean, and fake bars and baroque music that never stops. If only I'd married you and lived here—"

"You could have," Jules said. He saw the pile of engagement presents in Bessy's parents' apartment and shuddered. Silver trays and toast racks—and his own present to Bessy, the famous yellow diamond that had caused all the trouble in the end. The crowded courtroom, Bessy's breach-of-promise suit, the charges he had brought against her in turn. "No one likes to be publicly branded as impotent," he said when the vision had faded.

"I could hardly have lived with you without sex!" Bessy cried. "Think of what all my friends would have said!"

Jules swung down from the hammock and stood staring at the facade of the manor, so soon to be no more than a tourist attraction with his own body lying inert in one of the refurbished rooms. He sighed.

"To this day I tell people you were never a homosexual," Bessy insisted. "They say you're suffering from paranoia, you know, that you imagine all the time that people are coming to kill you. I say nonsense!"

"Perhaps it's true." Jules yawned. "Look, Bessy, there's a strange little man standing on the front doorstep. He seems to be dressed for the racetrack at Ascot. I wonder who it can be?"

Bessy crawled to the edge of the carpet and peered. She gave a low gasp. "It's the man I saw in the Quarter earlier today! We all thought there was something suspicious about him. He must be—the detective, Jules."

"His hat's in rather bad shape," Jules remarked.

Haines followed the winsome, aged couple (despite their years they were a good deal taller than he was, and he was forced to go through a reverse process of his experience in the country lane, feeling every moment more shrunken as he trailed after them) through the empty, stuccoed rooms of Woodiscombe Manor. Silently he wondered what had become of all the furniture, and what the reactions of the Department would be when he explained that the stately home was no longer England's last treasure house. There were, he noted with anxiety, practically no relics of the great heritage of the past—except for the victim himself, and Jules looked almost too eccentric to pass for a suitable body. Haines, coming to a halt by an unmovable suit of armor in the old dining room, tried to summon up the courage to demand that Jules's dusty red hair be cut—it was piled in a chignon and held unsteadily with a Spanish comb—and that the facial makeup be cleansed. But Jules had hardly drawn breath since the beginning of the tour.

"This is the room where Gertrude Stein and I discussed *Tender Buttons*. Oddly enough it's the very room where Edith Wharton told me she was in love with Henry James and said she had told him he had to get rid of his drunken servants if she was ever to visit him again. Isn't that an amusing coincidence?"

Haines gave a grim nod. He had not only erased his own memories, but, since he had in any case forgotten his literary education, found he had no memories on these subjects to erase. All he knew was that Bessy Pontoon, the obvious suspect, the suspect he had been warned would be considered too obvious to be acceptable, was standing with her arm in Jules's and looking murderously up at him. Haines trembled lest the crime should take place that very evening, before he had time to unpack his kit and question the victim. This was too much! He cursed at her unwelcome presence on the scene of the crime.

"And here is the library," said Jules with a slight tremor in his voice. He turned for the first time to Haines, smiling so fulsomely that Haines instantly guessed his attention was being diverted.

"My poor Mr. Haines! You haven't unpacked yet and here I am exhausting you with a tour of the house! Bessy, go and find Sing and tell him to bring us cocktails. At once!"

"Sing is the butler?" said Haines tonelessly.

"Oh, not a real one," said Jules, laughing. "Not the sort of butler who finds . . . not a butler out of mystery stories, I can assure you." His laugh grew more high-pitched. "I was expecting you to bring a butler with you, Mr. Haines."

Haines held out his empty hands and explained that his luggage was in the Buick. Not that he would be needing much for the remaining two days, of course. His detective kit he carried on his person.

"How silly of me!" A tear glinted in the corner of Jules's eye. "Two days, no, you'd hardly need more than a change of clothes, would you? And I'm sure Sing can fit you out with something."

Bessy, who had gone to summon the cocktails, reappeared clapping her hands girlishly.

"Real alcohol here, Jules, darling! What a full cellar

you must have had at the time of the Revolution!"

Haines gave no sign of reacting to this. He pulled a tape measure from his inside pocket and went to kneel in a far corner of the room. Both Jules and Bessy watched him in silence for a while as he drew the tape to the center of the carpet and scribbled something in a notebook. He looked up once, to see Sing's brown naked feet shuffle past. Two glasses gaily banged against each other.

"Won't you have one, Mr. Haines?"

Haines said he wouldn't. He reached into his pocket again and drew out a piece of chalk, white and firm, never before used. On the center of the carpet he drew an X, then rolled up the tape neatly and restored it to its hiding place. Slightly flushed, he rose to his feet.

"I'd like to see my accommodation, if I might, Mr. Tanner."

Jules, slopping his martini as he walked, approached the white cross and stared down at it. Bessy gave a low laugh.

"Where the body will be situated," said Haines when Jules asked him the question. "Visible from windows back and front, allowing for side ropes."

"Of course! How silly of me," Jules said after a short pause.

9

Breakfast with the Suspects

Haines slept badly in what had once been known as the Maple Room. (Faded gilt lettering on the door proclaimed this, and the bellpull by the decaying four-poster was connected with a tocsin in the basement labeled with the same words. Haines, in one of his instantly forgotten dreams, had tugged at the tassel and Jules had awakened, two floors down, his heart jumping with fear.) Haines came down to breakfast to find Jules at an oak table in the morning room, bacon and eggs set out before him on a hot plate. There was as yet no sign of Bessy.

"Sing and I brought the table up from the cellar at my father's insistence," Jules said when Haines had offered a curt good-morning. "As you can see, he's not down to breakfast yet, which is most unlike him.

I'm beginning to wonder whether one oughtn't to go to his room and see if my father's had a stroke in his sleep or something."

Haines looked warily down the table. Apart from his place and Jules's, four settings, each complete with lacy place mats and crested knives and spoons, sat unused on the polished surface. Massive chairs with tortuously carved backs stood by, awaiting their occupants. It occurred to Haines that Sing and Jules between them must have worked hard in the night to restore these monsters to their rightful place. He cleared his throat and sat down opposite Jules, helping himself to the plentiful breakfast food of the past.

"You are expecting visitors?" Haines, munching toast, assumed the casual tone of one house-party guest inquiring after the others (a bridge hand among them, perhaps, or an ace tennis player) but in spite of his disturbing night he had swung his faculties into top speed, and was calculating the possible reasons for this intimation of an already populated house. It was the last thing he had expected. That Jules would pick his murderer from a list of agreed suspects, and that Haines, in a televised summing-up in the library, would prove brilliantly to the world how the crime had been committed and (trick ending) by the most improbable person, he had assumed and prepared for. But if the murder was already planned, and without his permission—

"We must have a discussion," Haines added before Jules had time to answer his question.

"Ah, here they are," cried Jules, waving his hand in greeting. "Mr. Haines, allow me the pleasure of introducing you. My father, Sir Clovis Tanner. Doctor David Makins. And Bessy you have already met."

Bessy this morning was wearing a nearly opaque negligee, the swirling chiffon embroidered with dragons and serpents which floated, fiery nostrils uppermost, around her ample body. A strong smell of perfume mingled with the bacon and eggs.

Haines gazed anxiously at the door—green baize on the far side, walnut this side—but it had swung shut again. Bessy, showing no signs of recognizing or not recognizing the other guests, began to eat greedily.

"Pass the marmalade to Sir Clovis, please, Mr. Haines," said Jules. "He doesn't usually talk at breakfast, you know. Afterward you must ask David about his experiences in Indochina. He can tell you every possible disease of the liver one can contract in that awful place. And the little worm—hookworm, is it, David—that enters by the sole of the foot and eats its way upward? Leaving little for those who come later, I believe?"

Haines fiddled with his already crumpled and soiled tie and smiled cunningly across the table at Jules.

"Bessy Pontoon is here on a purely social visit, I take it?" he asked in his flattest, most menacing tone.

"I would very much like to hear how Miss Pontoon intends to pass her time here."

Bessy looked up impatiently from her third helping of cold pheasant breast, and with a lacquered nail pressed the table bell for more coffee. Sing came in noiselessly and filled all the cups but one from a silver pot. Jules, with a sigh of contentment, leaned back in his chair and wiped his lips.

Haines tried again. "And who are we waiting for?" he said pleasantly, pointing at the empty cup. "I had no idea, Mr. Tanner, that you already had invited most of the suspects to Woodiscombe."

"There was no need," Bessy said through a mouthful of cold ham. "I came down to help Jules myself. The most painless way—and the most romantic."

"And what would that be?" Haines said. He made a mental note to get Bessy out of the place by the end of the morning, using official means if necessary. They had, after all, made it more or less clear that the choice of Bessy would be a disappointment to them. Quickly he must find the perfect assortment of suspects, send for them wherever they might be, construct and destroy alibis for the expectant public. He signaled to Jules that the time had come for the two of them to get down to business alone.

"We're waiting for Cedric," Jules said. "David, I don't think you ever met Cedric, did you? No, of course you didn't. I'm afraid Father never approved of him much, did you, Father? Cedric, Mr. Haines, is one of the great actors of the century. Which century are we in anyway? No matter. The legend of Cedric will never die, Mr. Haines. He is a true professional. Joined the chorus of *Lilac Time* when he had to pay his debts. Gave the most brilliant rendering of Claudius in the history of the stage. And he was in the feminist production of *Othello*, playing Othello as a white man. Surely you have thrilled to Cedric's performances, Mr. Haines?"

Bessy had finally finished her meal. "A suicide pact," she said dreamily, fixing her once-limpid gaze on the detective. "Jules and I will go together, an empty vial found by our side. Where do you think, Jules? In the waterfall garden perhaps—or in bed?"

Jules grimaced and rose from the table. He pulled a selection of thin, yellow paperbacks from the shelf behind him and flicked one open, frowning down at the cheap quality of the paper and crude, smudged print.

"If there's one thing about your new Government, Mr. Haines, that I think I must complain about, it's the revolting literature one gets issued with nowadays. Is this what children are taught in schools? Are these the classics of the future? Just listen to this—"

Haines's mind raced as Jules read aloud. A suicide pact—impossible! Totally unacceptable to the overseas visitors, accustomed as they were to mass suicide in the West. And the Department! Haines shuddered at the thought of the reaction there. He would be demoted, no question of that. If not worse. With a great effort Haines summoned the healing crossword puzzle once more. Jules read on.

> Ursula and Gudrun, deep in the blinding snows, overpowered by the snow which fell around them like a great feather quilt, watched Raskolnikov as he came toward them, knife in hand. Maggie Verver and the Prince were but a few steps behind him.

Jules broke off and fixed Haines with an accusing stare. "What is this hodge-podge, Mr. Haines? I see here in what they term the explanatory preface that novels may only be written now which contain already established characters. Is this true? Are there no characters of today?"

Haines rose. He glared discouragingly at Bessy, whose gold dragons were now in midair as she pulled herself up to join him, and she subsided once more, pressing the bell for Sing to bring her a drink.

"There are no memories today," Haines said. "Observations of present-day life are disallowed. Therefore it was considered expedient and economical to utilize already existing characters."

"And novels about the future?" cried Jules.

"These would be speculative, thus unconvincing. It is a pure waste of time to invent characters and situations which do not yet, and may never, exist. Now, Mr. Tanner, I think we had better have our little talk."

Jules bowed in the direction of the other places at the long table.

"We will meet at lunch, Father. Why not try a game of chess with David? He plays very well, or so I've been told."

Haines followed Jules into the library.

10

Cedric's Discovery

It was often said by the pundits—those who theorized on behavior patterns in the new environment, studied memory loss in the old, put the works of Shakespeare on microfilm and suchlike—that there existed three categories of persons. The first adapted totally to present circumstances; the second were able only to adapt with half of themselves, so to speak; and the third were incapable of adapting at all.

This fable, charmingly reminiscent of Goldilocks and the Three Bears, was put forward as an explanation of the "uneven society" of the times: the crowd fitted neatly into the third category, and it was doomed, because of its inability to grasp the consequences of the new conditions, to an endless cycle of births and early deaths, poverty, and archaic, rapidly subdued attempts at balkanization and self-government; the second (into which, as we shall see, poor Haines plunged headlong) consisted of those who understood the conditions, obeyed the orders, but found themselves finally unable to bear the life-style they had once welcomed; and the first, to which Cedric Brown definitely belonged, included scientists, professors, and members of the Government.

The gap between the groups widened yearly, and the reason given for this was that never before in history had there been so many changes made at such speed. Only those with excellent digestions could swallow a society that altered daily—so said the pundits, though many felt that life now consisted, more than ever, of more of the same.

These, then, were labeled third category—the hippies of the past, the ex-working class—and left, as nonsurvivors, to live out their unmodern existence as best they could.

Unfortunately, and this was an embarrassment to the professors and the Government, a handful of clever people survived who often found themselves in disagreement with the theory. These people were bribed by every means available to keep quiet and not upset the balance, unbalanced though it was. They were offered top advisory jobs and diplomatic posts, the running of banks, and positions that would satisfy the remnants of their idealism, like Minister of Housing and Undersecretary for Public Health.

All of these Cedric Brown had refused; and as a

result he was watched carefully by the other members of the first category. The only reason he had not yet been eliminated was because he might prove valuable one day—but this was no longer thought likely in high places. As a punishment for his noncooperation he had been selected for the most frivolous end imaginable. He guessed this one fine late April morning while listening to the radio—and laughed quietly to himself before adjusting the dial to a Bach and Mozart concert. Sometimes, he was forced to concede, the Government was capable of displaying a macabre sense of humor.

No one seeing Cedric Brown for the first time would have considered him a potential menace to society. Like most actors he had a kind of nonface, a rubbery stretch of skin like an old canvas that has been painted over by several artists in succession and still shows traces of the landscape or portrait beneath. He had given up acting at the time of the Revolution (it was he, of course, who had captured all the great parts in the expensive revivals and dreary modern plays of the time, not Jules, with his captive audience of Sing and an imagination-packed proscenium), but when the Revolution came—and Cedric was most in demand to play the lead in the new Revolutionary plays—he had turned them all down and gone to live in the Hermitage, a complex of white, tomblike buildings on a promontory in Cornwall. He had no intention of declaiming the stale orations concocted by the new

Government to bus loads of tourists; besides, he had other interests he wanted to develop. One of these was astronomy.

Princes Point, the away-from-it-all retreat of the privileged and famous, made a perfect base for Cedric's new interest. He fixed up a powerful telescope, ordered books on the subject from America, and settled down to study the sky. Rumors went around to the effect that his villa had been turned into a laboratory, and that he was inventing a cheap cure for boredom and lethargy, but the latter was certainly not the case. Cedric felt no concern for the problems of others, and he cared little for his own survival. He refused to commit suicide, an expedient which had become devalued by too-frequent use. But he knew that within a matter of months he would be able to understand the universe—and this pleased him.

On that late April morning, while Haines was poring over Jules's old letters and journals, while Jules was reaching the conclusion that it would be a sad thing to die, and was on the brink of offering the detective Woodiscombe and all its contents for another week of old age, while Bessy was preparing a vial of cyanide, vodka, and consommé, and was deciding to forget the suicide pact, to give the mixture to Jules alone, while the crowd thronged restlessly on the beach below Princes Point and new hotels were going up on the remaining land in readiness for the summer visitors,

Cedric made a surprising discovery. He wandered, dazed, away from the telescope, then checked and rechecked his graphs. He whistled through his teeth, helped himself to a strong whisky, sent free to residents of Princes Point, and splashed in some soda.

He had no desire to confide his discovery to anyone, for he had lived alone for a long time now. But the result of his research was too staggering to take in all at once. He flicked on the radio (TV was nothing but Revolutionary soap operas these days) and sat down.

Cedric had seen that there was no universe at all. There was the sun; and Earth, of course, with its billions of inhabitants dreaming of the day when it would be possible to find space again by flying off to the distant planets, settling, colonizing and marking out a territory the very concept of which had vanished at home—and there was the moon, as the astronauts had proved. And there was nothing else!

The stars were optical illusions, products of the human eye; reflections from the retina, a fault in man's makeup. You could close your eyes and see stars and planets as real as those charted over the past millennia by earnest astronomers. The pinpricks of light in the eyes of a cat at night were more tangible than Mars or Saturn, the Milky Way a corneal smudge, a blur in vision that could be wiped away, like an insect which had flown in by mistake, with a handkerchief. It was a horrible discovery.

Cedric went back into his laboratory and stared down for a moment at the trays of eyes, some shining, some dull, the blues set out in a line above the browns like an arrangement of butterflies—then tipped them into the incinerator. He returned to his chair and helped himself to another drink. It was at that point that he began to hear what was being said on the radio.

"Among other attractions, the Queen will make an appearance on the balcony of Buckingham Palace. Closed-circuit systems in the principal hotels will provide close-ups of our monarch and her family . . . the new Loch Ness development is completed this month, the slum clearance having been successful, and visitors to the hotels there will be able to view the monster in glass-bottomed platforms built out over the lake—sorry, Macs, loch . . . an item causing much excitement and amusement is the last country house murder, planned for May 1 to enable west-bound tourist traffic to make a stopover at Stonehenge. . . . Clearances under way there now, accommodation completed by April 30, how's that for getting the crowd out from under your feet and gorgeous new hotels up in record time? . . . What was that I was saying, Jimmy? Oh yes . . . to enable Wessex-bound tourists to make a stopover before going on to the Cheddar and Dorset Oil Developments. . . . Our detective Lord Peter Wimsey cracks the murder mystery at Woodiscombe, the body in the library being none other than a certain Jules Tanner, last of the landed rich. Now for OUR latest piece of detection, a singer you may all have heard of lately, the glorious . . ."

Cedric pushed the knob to Bach and continued to sit thoughtfully in his chair. After a while he rose and went out to his terrace, which was the roof of the house below him on the sloping promontory. He looked down at the necropolis of beehive-shaped houses, the crowds that poured over the distant cliffs, and up at the starless sky. With a shrug of resignation he climbed into his white helicopter and set the automatic pilot to West Wiltshire.

11

Haines Investigates

"So it's all yours," said Jules. "I'll make a will, everything aboveboard and all that. It's just that I do want to see the syringa in bloom one more time. It comes out in the first week of May, I can't tell you what a beautiful sight it is. Wouldn't YOU like to see it, dear Mr. Haines?"

"I will be seeing it," Haines said. The two men were sitting cross-legged on the floor of the library, the ominous chalk mark between them. A pile of letters and journals had accumulated at Haines's side. "Anyway," he added, "the Government disallows inherited wealth. I'm afraid your last will and testament would be meaningless, Mr. Tanner."

"What nonsense!" Jules cried. "You mean one can't leave one's things to—to someone one has come to love? And esteem," he went on not very convincingly. "All the stuff's in the cellar, you know. Yours in exchange for the first week in May; not a bad deal when you come to think of it."

Haines smiled contemptuously and continued to sift through the debris of Jules's life. A faded gold-edged card crept into his hand and he glanced at it, puzzled at first by the quirky, pretentious writing. It said:

Crudités
Le Potage du Jour
Medaillons de Veau Rothschild
Compôte de Fruits
Présenté par le Chef de Brigade Marly

Jules snatched it, his attention diverted for a moment. "The very last Golden Arrow menu, Mr. Haines. That was a historic trip. But I must say they might have taken more trouble with the food. It was disgusting."

"Ah!" Haines brightened at the sight of what was clearly a very angry letter. Starting in typescript, it ran after a few closely spaced lines into cheap ballpoint, the dotted i's like thunderclouds on the thin, lined paper. Shutting his ears to Jules's reminiscences of famous train journeys, Haines read carefully. The letter was headed "Parkhurst."

Dear Jules,

I have borrowed this typewriter from one of the Kray brothers, who has been kind enough to lend me various essentials during my stay here. Here he is and I must give it back to him so I will continue in pen. I hope you realize what you have done to me, Jules. My life is wrecked, my career finished, my prospects nonexistent and Flora left me immediately after the trial. I know I shouldn't have taken the money but, Jules, I needed it desperately and quite honestly what difference did it make to you? I got the impression that pure spite prompted your actions. All right, there were false pretenses but not as false as you think. I felt no revulsion for you, I can swear that—I was bisexual at school. Here they refuse to give me the diet I need for my illness. I suppose they want me to die, and so do you. So does Flora now, probably. We were so in love with each other and I had a practice fixed up at Sheen for when we were married. Never mind. I'm just writing to say I would be very grateful if you could get in touch with the prison authorities and remind them about my diet. The Governor is deaf to my pleas. Jules, you owe me this if nothing more.

DAVID

"And it used to be fun at the French Embassy," Jules was saying. "The *crème caramel* was superb, one felt one was floating up to heaven while one was eating it."

"Did you remind the prison authorities about this young man's diet?" Haines said severely. "Where is he now, please, Mr. Tanner?"

Jules ran a hand through his piled hair. "I'm afraid they weren't interested in his diet at all. I sent in a hamper from Fortnum and Mason, but I gather the Krays took it."

"And where is he now?"

"David was at breakfast, Mr. Haines. You were a little rude to him, I thought, ignoring him like that."

Haines gave a snort of exasperation. He filed the letter and rummaged through the papers again, fishing up a fragment of thick parchment covered with thick Victorian writing. Jules moaned playfully. "That's my father's hand, you know. That black ink he used! I used to wake in the night screaming when I thought of it. Don't read it!"

Haines read aloud:

> My dear son,
>
> You have been a disappointment to me in many ways, but this latest scandal has proved the last-straw. To be sacked from Eton is a disgrace, and I intend to apply a fitting punishment. The own-

> ership of Woodiscombe, as you know, is up to me. I have therefore decided to leave the place to your cousin Anthony. He is coming in the long vacation for some shooting, and your presence here would be most unwelcome. I enclose £10 for your expenses, to cover the months July, August, and September.
>
> YOUR FATHER

"So the place isn't yours to dispose of," said Haines. "Not that the Government—"

"No, no, they don't allow it, I know," Jules said eagerly. "So you ARE considering the offer, Mr. Haines. How sensible of you! Of course, that was only a threat from Father; as you could see at breakfast he's the most genial chap possible, really."

Haines thought for a moment.

"If Sir Clovis is alive," he remarked, "then Woodiscombe isn't yours to leave to anyone. I think you're getting yourself in quite a tangle, and had better come clean now."

With these menacing words Haines rose and went over to the window, one of the journals in his hand. He scanned the multicolored tropical flowers that danced in the margin of Jules's entry for June 12, 1929, and saw:

> My resolution for today—always travel alone; let

> the trip with Bessy be a lesson to me. I shall certainly get the ring back; how very vulgar of her to keep it. How tired and strained I look! Try out the lovely new Elizabeth Arden pack . . . . . . possibly add mud from garden. If the eyebrows were stronger would the balance of my face go? I wonder. Garbo's eyebrows haunt.

"Woodiscombe was made over to me, of course," Jules was saying impatiently. "How ignorant you are, my dear. Have you never heard of death duties?"

"So Sir Clovis died," said Haines.

"I told you, he was at breakfast," Jules replied. He pulled himself up from the floor with some difficulty and went to peer over Haines's shoulder. "Oh, you're reading that one. The ring! It was quite a court case, I must say. The Majipore diamond. Yellow, like a tiger's eye." Jules gave Haines's shoulder an affectionate pat. "I bet the Government is looking forward to getting its hands on that! Would you like to see it, Mr. Haines? I keep it in a very special part of the cellar."

"I can so far find no references to the Cedric you mentioned, Mr. Tanner. Can you tell my why you selected him, please?"

Jules clasped his hands together under his chin as he examined his reflection in the mirror.

"Would you like to OWN the ring, Mr. Haines? Do come and see it anyway."

12

The Diamond

Something—some mocking chromosome, a mismatched pair of genes perhaps, one harking back to the acquisitive instincts of the past, the other straining ahead to the propertyless future—or a forgotten environmental factor such as the time Haines accompanied his parents on a visit to a shop selling unclaimed lost property and saw the rows of umbrellas, dank scarves, and old schoolbags, each marked with the sadness of having once belonged to someone—something of that nature lay at the roots of Haines's inevitable corruption. He was not aware at first of the process, though in some buried area of his mind he was already fighting it vigorously. Afterward, in the few seconds granted him to review his life, he saw the progression, like a thin string pulling him in one direction as he marched bravely off in the other, and the impossibility, at any stage, of severing himself from it. But by then, of course, it was too late for further reflection.

The diamond was the size of a gull's egg. Years in a black box had in no way affected its powerful beam. It caught the light from the miserable bulb in the cellar, trapped it in its tawny depths and transformed it into a million rays of dazzling, blinding energy. It became the source of light and energy itself—the paintings and carpets and objects around which Haines stumbled in Jules's wake were dim things, deadened, not brought to life by its renewed existence. However hard Haines tried, his eyes were drawn from the contemplation of a portrait, his mind from the recognition of the famous treasures, by the glimmering earth star on its piece of dusty velvet. It made him thirsty, and quenched his thirst at the same time. It followed him around the room like a malign, jubilant eye.

Haines went thoughtfully back to the library when the inspection was over. Jules, in order to demonstrate the pathos of his situation, wandered in the garden under the library windows. For a long time Haines sifted methodically through the correspondence and journals while the diamond, two floors below, shone unseen. It hung, imprinted on his inner eye, over the tattered expressions of long-forgotten love and disguised malice.

With no feeling of surprise Haines filed a letter from the prison authorities saying that Dr. David Makins had died of diabetes on August 15, and would Mr. Tanner care to collect his effects. A memorial service card for Sir Clovis was marked May 1, 1928. Another May-day death for his son; but Haines felt no interest at the coincidence. He arranged photographs of the Siamese twins Dora and Violet naked on a bearskin rug (studio shot, their faces slightly blurred, their four legs tastefully side by side) and collected evidence on two young men, Simon and Jimmy, who penned blackmailing letters to the victim from the Berlin of prewar years.

The diamond grew in size as Haines worked, becoming first a great stretch of parkland where Haines walked alone, the crowds as many miles away as the perimeter of the diamond; then an island, a glittering haven in an unpopulated sea; then England itself, empty, beautiful and his. Haines untied a faded red ribbon around a bunch of letters and they crumbled to dust like ancient papyruses. Uncaring, he swept the debris into a corner of the room. The chalkmark on the carpet looked innocently up at him as he passed.

At this point Jules called up from the garden. Haines, glancing nervously at the cross on the floor, went to the window and pushed it open. Jules had changed into an Indian robe of antique splendor and was leaning on the stone parapet by the goldfish pond, his attitude that of a young poet contemplating death. Bessy swung of a hammock in the background.

"Cedric's letters are in the Chinese lacquer box," Jules shouted. "It'll save you time, Mr. Haines. You're thinking over my offer, I hope?"

Haines closed the window and went slowly back to the monstrous assortment. The Chinese box lay under a mausoleum of wedding invitations and dance cards, stiff cardboard menus, and old periodicals. It opened without a key. As Haines read, the diamond faded a little and the reality of his task presented itself once more; with a dry bureaucrat's cough he spread the letters around him and took out his pen for notes.

Even Haines could see that Cedric was a man of genius, and therefore a threat to the State, Haines's employers, and benefactors. Many of the advanced mathematical allusions were incomprehensible—and some of the letters were written entirely in symbols. The references to Art (" . . . I have invented the painting of the future, the camera which records not what it sees but what is about to happen: a time-warp that brings the imprint of the future to the present—imagine, dear Jules, a busy street which is about to be suddenly vacated, emptiness superimposed on the what-is-already-here") left Haines cold. Cedric's descriptions of his acting career he skimmed over. But the casual mentions of Cedric's political beliefs Haines immediately recognized as dangerous. In shockingly flippant style, Cedric described various successful methods of bringing down the present Government and restoring anarchy in its place. Unbelievably casual . . . wicked . . . Haines shrank back—like a priest finding himself at a Black Mass. He collected the letters, put them back in the box, and went down the stairs holding it out in front of him as if it contained a spiteful adder. All was clear now—why the official at headquarters had warned him against Bessy as murderer, what the real reason for this charade must be. How clever! Haines thrilled for a moment at the ingeniousness of the massed minds in the Department. A fitting, scornful gesture—and a way of getting rid of a potential public enemy without agitating the people. If Cedric wished to indulge his vengeful instincts and come and kill an old friend—what better way than of using a personal quarrel for the common good.

Haines reached the bottom of the stairs, his mind already made up. Time was short. He must find this man, engineer him into a situation where he killed (or appeared to kill, Haines had no scruples about administering a fatal dose to Jules himself), and was subsequently, after several red herrings, found guilty. Minor characters flashed through Haines's mind, a hodge-podge from the journals. He began to deduce and calculate. More suspects would have to be rushed down to the manor today. He snapped their names into the tiny cassette player. With a confident step he strode through the hall and swung open the door leading to the garden. The diamond flashed once before his eyes and disappeared again.

David Makins and Sir Clovis Tanner were sitting on the stone seat by the goldfish pond. They seemed to be deep in conversation with each other. Jules joined in from time to time, then resumed his poetic stance. Bessy dozed in the hammock. Haines put out a terrified hand to the climbing vine. Recoiling from the clammy touch of the plastic, he staggered back into the hall.

"Ah, Mr. Haines," called Jules. "Come and have a little chat before lunch."

13

Old Movies

Cedric sat at the controls of his white helicopter. From time to time he remembered his recent discovery and smiled to himself; but his mind was already occupied with other matters. It was a long time since he had last left the sanctuary of Princes Point, and what he saw beneath him filled him with horror. Vague stirrings of conscience returned to him at the sight of the crowded tenement towns, overspills which spilled over into each other in the wild lateral rush for accommodation, the islands of high-rise buildings which stood out like the jawbones of prehistoric animals in the despoiled landscape.

It was clear that the last few years had produced neither kindness nor any coherent form of planning policy on the part of the Government; on the contrary, freedom to live had turned to freedom to die, for it seemed unlikely that mankind could survive for long in such conditions. Cedric thought of the camera he had once invented, and in his mind transformed the debris below into an architectural dream, where buildings of soaring beauty stood surrounded by the soft greenness of parks, and people, their sanity restored by fine proportions and evenly distributed wealth, lived happily ever after. But his camera was only capable of seeing the immediate future—and even if the length of the time-warp could be increased, there was no guarantee that this dream would ever be realized. So much needed to be erased by now, to make such a future possible.

Cedric pondered, and set the automatic pilot for landing. To find a space large enough on the uplands needed the accuracy of the computer; for as far as the human eye could see there was no suitable space anywhere. The few remaining plowed fields were too muddy. The roofs of the wooden skyscrapers looked about as safe as coming down on a pack of cards. He descended slowly, looking out for the first glimpse of the chimney stacks of Woodiscombe Manor.

The crowd below spotted the helicopter, and wave after wave of people poured out of the temporary buildings to stare up at it. The Government helicopters were red, so no cry for cover went up. Cedric was conscious of a great silence as the needle of the pilot swung uncertainly, and finally guided the machine to a grassy burial mound about twenty feet high. No building had as yet been erected on it, but planks of wood and makeshift scaffolding lay at the base. The crowd pressed around expectantly. Cedric pushed open the hatch and stepped out.

It was then that the once-famous actor found himself possessed of a rage which he had thought long buried and forgotten since the Revolution. If he was to die—obediently, at the wish of others, and because there was little point, he had to concur, in his continued existence—then he would make one last gesture before he went.

To go and murder an old friend! For the sake of the tourist trade, while the crowd starved and died! He would obey, out of consideration for Jules: together they could concoct an amusing and painless end, and he would kill himself when the crime was "discovered," in the manner of many detective story villains. He had no intention of enduring a mock trial, imprisonment and probable death by hanging for the extended delight of the overseas visitors. But he could perhaps make things a little difficult—

The closest observer would have found it hard to say what Cedric did when he stepped from the helicopter and stood, the wind blowing at his hair, on the grassy ledge above the crowd. His features simply moved—a fraction of an inch here, a slight droop about the mouth, a slouch in the shoulders. A roar of instant recognition went up.

"It's Bogart! It's Bogie!"

Hands reached up to him, smiles broke out on sullen faces. From the long years of apathy and deprivation, with the only diversion old movies and intolerable soap operas, the hero had come at last to the rescue. A dizzy lightness seized the crowd, who knew by now every nuance in every scene of all the pre-seventies movies ever made.

"The last scene from *Casablanca!*"

"Bogie, light a cigarette!"

"Can't you see the bulge of the gun in his raincoat?"

A babble of Hindi, South London, West Indian and Liverpool filled the air. Women screamed as Cedric depressed his lower lip in the gangster's smile. Children scrambled up the bank and tugged at his trouser legs.

A slight facial twitch and there was another roar of appreciation. The hunted, evil face of Fagin hung over the crowd. "Kill him! Lynch him!" came the chorus. "Fagin for our leader! Down with the New Government!"

Cedric paused a moment, invisibly removing the character of Fagin and leaving in its place a bland, smallish man with no characteristics at all. The crowd gasped at the transformation. An expectant hush fell. One voice—a man's, deep-throated—shouted: "It's Cedric Brown! Up with Cedric Brown! Get us out of this mess, Cedric!"

Cedric swung his arm out in front of him. His rubbery, mobile face grew suddenly thinner, his eyes pierced the crowd. A low moan rippled among the ranks of jostling people, many of them standing on each other's shoulders, then clambering down and changing places so that all could witness the extraordinary apparition. Something in Cedric's stance brought a new rigidity to the crowd, which formed into lines miles long, bodies stiff and upright. A great army had sprung from the ground. Cedric opened his mouth—and shouted. The roar of acclaim that greeted him was different in tone from the previous ones: the crowd was shouting in unison now, and with increased vigor.

"Mein Führer!"

Cedric walked slowly down from the heights of the burial mound and through the serried ranks of waiting troops. His gait was contained and menacing. A whimper of fear went up from some children, who were clinging to the skirts of their saluting mothers. Ah, that had been his very best role, the crowning moment of his career! The crowd would do anything he wanted now; they waited, they only waited for his command. He stopped at the center of the massed parade and raised himself a couple of feet above the crowd by stepping onto a wooden crate marked "Government Supplies." He spoke, in a thundering voice that carried as far as the line of trees which marked the end of the uplands and the precincts of Woodiscombe Manor.

"You will receive a smoke signal from the chimneys of that great house! Then—march on Parliament!"

"Ja, Führer!"

The crowd stood rigid as Cedric marched down the hill. He disappeared between the trees and pressed the bell at the manor gate. It swung open and he walked down the drive, Cedric again. The distant crowd broke into song behind him.

14

Haines Meets His Past

"What noise they're making today," Jules complained. "Have a Scotch and soda, Mr. Haines. Most delicious at this hour, I always find."

Haines, who had been cajoled out into the garden with some difficulty, sat uneasily between Sir Clovis and the young doctor on the stone seat. Jules, reminiscing about his engagement to Bessy, had run into the house to get the diamond, and it burned now on the grass under the hammock, giving off a smoky radiance which appeared to be unnoticed by all but Haines. He eyed it apprehensively, allowing himself only the smallest of small talk with his neighbors.

Now that Haines was sitting with them, Jules was pretending to ignore them altogether, and he had even on a couple of occasions reprimanded Haines for talking to himself. Haines felt he was on the point of going mad. A few basics remained with him. He remembered that at breakfast he had decided to get Bessy out of the place as soon as possible—but then, surely, he had made a note to the effect that a lot more people must be invited as suspects to Woodiscombe?

Bessy, so far, was showing every symptom of a murderer planning a crime; she was silent and contemplative in her hammock, emitting from time to time a vengeful and bitter snort of laughter. A glass containing the poisonous mixture she had made up for Jules stood by the diamond on the grass beneath her swinging body. Haines knew he must find Cedric, but had lost the confidence to ask Jules how to set about it. For the time, Jules definitely had the upper hand.

"I won't drink your horrible concoction," he was saying, as Haines sat on, head lowered. "For one thing, I much prefer Scotch and soda. And dear Mr. Haines here is giving me an extra beautiful week of life in exchange for the Majipore stone. Isn't that sensible of him?"

Sir Clovis tapped Haines playfully on the shoulder. "I believe people can change their ways, don't you, Mr. Haines? You see, my feelings for Jules are as follows: He is my son and I have given him everything a fond parent could possibly give his heir, the apple of his eye. But is the line to end with him? Am I to go to my grave with that knowledge? Of course, some boys, I know, do go through a phase . . . In short, Mr. Haines, if Jules were to marry now—and I'm not saying I ever approved of the Pontoon family, but it can't be helped at this stage—then I would see things in a very different light. What do you think of that?"

Haines shrank back from Sir Clovis' bearded face and strong smell of decomposition, and murmured, "I think you're right there, Sir Clovis."

His mind was spinning, but something in Sir Clovis's speech made sense. If Bessy were reconciled with Jules, then she would be unlikely to try and murder him while he, Haines, laid out the clues and instigated a search for the approved suspect.

"That's a very good idea, Sir Clovis," Haines continued. The diamond sent a shaft of light into his eyes as he spoke and he closed them again with a low groan.

"Poor Mr. Haines has inherited my guilty past," said Jules gaily. "The wonderful thing is, Bessy, that every since he came out into the garden those boring ghosts have vanished. For me, I mean. Mr. Haines is saddled with them for life, I fear."

Bessy pushed her legs over the side of the hammock and glared at Jules. "What do you mean you're giving my engagement ring to Mr. Haines? How dare you? It's mine."

"We went through all that in court," Jules reminded her. "And they gave the stone back to me. Don't say you can't remember!"

David Makins sighed heavily in Haines's left ear. His physiognomy, shriveled as it was by two years in prison, resembled that of a stuffed monkey Haines had seen on his unfortunate and formative visit to the lost property shop. Other aspects of him, too, brought back a flood of forbidden memories: the stovepipe trousers were identical to those worn by Haines's father in his younger days; the old-fashioned waterproof watch with the little button you pressed to time the school race—the very model proudly owned by Haines in his adolescence. It seemed, in fact (to Haines, in his miserable condition), that he had inherited not only Jules's phantoms but his own as well—his father's suffering face rose before him in place of the doctor's, his mother, heartrendingly patient, knelt on the grass at his feet and mended his tattered clothes. A vague but menacing line of men and women betrayed to authority by Haines at various stages of his life stretched out along the drive. He regarded them blankly, then saw that one of them was moving nearer, was assuming, in fact, the guise of each of Haines's past victims in turn. Haines felt himself tremble all over. The boy he had reported to the headmaster . . . the old man in his apartment block whom he had reported for making a secret collection of long-forgotten abstract paintings . . . the young mother he had found cheating Supplementary Benefit . . .

"I find it pretty disgusting, don't you?" David Makins was saying.

"What?" Haines, in his effort to avert his gaze from the approaching, ever-changing figure, looked straight into David's face and shuddered. Jules's guilt, however, was preferable to his own; and he concentrated as best he could.

"This talk of diamonds and lawsuits at a time when the world is starving. Do you know how many destitute Asians that stone would clothe and feed? How can you sit here and—and tolerate such a state of affairs?"

"This country is not responsible for the incompetence of other nations, Dr. Makins," said Haines. "And I am here only to fulfill my duties." (He noticed, to his intense annoyance, that his voice was shaking badly. His policy of disregarding the nonexistent stranger was doing no good, for he could now hear steps on the gravel.) Jules laughed.

"Here you are at last, Cedric! How lovely to see you. Bessy, of course, you remember. And this is Mr. Haines. He is a little indisposed this morning."

"Another example of the type of person this country can do well without," said David in his high-pitched, whining voice. "Lives entirely for his own amusement. There is no such thing as being nonpolitical, you know."

"There was a Revolution after you died," Haines snapped. "That type of person does not exist now. And if he does, the State sees to it that he is totally incapable of doing any harm."

"Poor Mr. Haines," said Jules. "You see what I mean,

Cedric. He's being plagued by a tiresome young doctor with a conscience whom I once met in Southeast Asia. What about a drink? I'll call Sing."

"Now who's this?" growled Sir Clovis. "Another of those annoying friends of Jules's, I suppose. You see, Mr. Haines, he's incorrigible. And I'd hoped—at this late stage—that he and Bessy—Is she past child-bearing, do you think, Mr. Haines?"

Jules laid a placating hand on Haines's arm.

"Do be polite and say hello to Cedric! He's come all this way—and he's just the man you wanted, you know. You're being a little ungrateful; it's Bessy who should be annoyed and not you. She was feeling so murderous, weren't you, darling?"

Haines rose numbly to his feet. He lifted his head as if it were a great weight that had suddenly descended on his shoulders and must be moved out of the way somehow. He stared at the direction from which the stranger's mumble of greeting had come. He saw a man of middle height, with no distinguishing marks, no resemblance to anyone he had ever known. Reluctantly, he nodded to him.

"I thought for a moment you were going to be silly and pretend not to see the people I saw, just because I can no longer see the people you see," Jules said, relieved. "I'll explain all this later, Cedric. Ah, here's Sing with a picnic lunch. Sit down, Cedric, and let's all help ourselves."

Haines looked on with horror as Cedric sat firmly down on Sir Clovis and began to talk about his life at Princes Point. With a malicious smile Jules pushed Haines back onto the seat—or rather onto David, who let out a squeal of protest. Cold chicken and mayonnaise wrapped in linen napkins was lifted from the hamper and handed around. Bessy, coaxed from the hammock, kicked over the poisonous drink as she stumbled onto the carpet laid down for her by Sing and, glowering, held out her champagne glass to be filled.

15

The Betrothal

After lunch Haines felt better, and he was even capable of dictating some notes on the coming case into his miniature recorder. Cedric was clearly no apparition; he produced a document, in the shape of a two-day-old postcard from an old friend (now in a high place in the Government), to prove his existence in the world; and Haines was suitably impressed and reassured.

As the memory of Sir Clovis and David faded, his mind began to function with its usual precision. He saw that Cedric's intelligent reading of the radio broadcast had brought him to Woodiscombe and that he had been saved the bother and anxiety of a search. All would go according to plan. Bessy provided the only stumbling block. Jules's assumption that Haines had accepted the diamond and had granted him an extra lease of life simply made him easier to murder.

Haines sipped at the champagne with pleasure and constructed the conversation he must have with Cedric. The diamond was safely in Haines's inside pocket. Bessy sat silent, eyes fixed on Haines's valuable chest.

"You know," Haines remarked in the nearest he could get to a debonair, conversational tone, "what this case needs is a little more excitement. Our overseas visitors must be confronted with as many suspects as possible. I told you, didn't I, Mr. Tanner, that we are having made a Solve-It-Yourself kit with earphones. As the tourists go around the house—"

"I don't think you did tell me," Jules replied in a haughty manner which Haines found ridiculous. Cedric's arrival seemed to have provided him with confidence rather than the opposite. Haines wondered if he was really aware of the purpose of Cedric's visit.

"On the closed-circuit screens will be clips of events leading up to the murder—"

"In a week's time," Jules said stiffly. "Or perhaps longer." He bit into a hothouse nectarine and giggled. Haines thought he saw Jules and Cedric exchange glances. His color rose.

"So it seemed to me a good idea if a wedding took place at Woodiscombe, Mr. Tanner."

A predictable silence followed. Haines thought quickly: If Cedric and Jules were planning some monkey business or other, trying to evade orders and escape unscathed from the situation, they would have to realize at once that this was out of the question. He added softly, "You do know we're all under surveillance here, Mr. Brown? There can be no permissible hitch, of course."

"A wedding!" Bessy sprang to her feet. "You mean me and Jules, Mr. Haines? I wouldn't dream of it! After all he's done to me in the past! All the humiliations, all the—"

"The diamond would be rightfully yours," Haines said, after a pause in which he appeared to consider the matter seriously. "I shouldn't say this, Miss Pontoon, but the Government is quite unaware of the existence of the diamond. It might prove very useful to you after Mr. Brown has . . . er . . . disposed of the matter in hand for us." He wiped his lips delicately with a napkin. "I would like to be remembered, of course—would count on your discretion—"

Bessy gave a loud laugh. She ran across the carpet and threw her arms around Jules's neck. Haines, conscious of Cedric's keen eyes on him, felt his heart leap under the hidden stone. He gazed thoughtfully down at his shoes, which were one spat short by now, and badly in need of a shine. He made a mental note to get Sing to tidy him up before the closed-circuit system was installed. And there was so much to do! Order the wedding guests, ask headquarters for workmen and engineers for TV and Sound. Lay the clues. The shadow on the sundial was lengthening. (His watch had stopped after breakfast and there was no other way of telling the time.) He must get on with things, and fast.

"If you insist," Jules was saying. "We might as well have our wedding at last, I suppose. Better fix the date. What about Friday next week?"

"Oh, no, Mr. Tanner. The wedding must take place tomorrow. I hope you understand that I am granting you another week and receiving as payment only a percentage of the diamond? This is because I feel that the stone belongs more to Miss Pontoon than it does to me."

"You can say that again!" Bessy chuckled with delight. "What a splendid idea, isn't it, Jules? So much more constructive than killing someone—marry them instead! Now, what on earth shall I wear? Are any of your mother's old dresses still here, Jules?"

"You certainly can't wear a dress of my mother's!" A tear rolled down Jules's cheek as he spoke. "I'm not sure I like that, Bessy!"

"If you'll forgive me, ladies and gentlemen. I have messages to transmit and work to do." Haines rose with dignity and made for the steps leading down from the raised garden to the drive. Bessy called out as he went.

"Can I have the diamond now, Mr. Haines?"

Haines turned and bowed, his full sense of officialdom restored.

"I'm afraid not, Miss Pontoon. We must film the betrothal, and the equipment has not yet arrived."

"But I want to celebrate now!"

Haines went steadily into the house and up the stairs, pausing to let out a deep breath when Cedric's wondering gaze was no longer on him. He was more tired than he thought and took the three flights to the attic with care, noting on the way the empty rooms which would have to be refurnished before the wedding and the squares of unfaded paint where once priceless pictures had hung. The long attic, when he had forced the door open, smelled of beeswax and dead flies. Haines pulled out his aerial and went over to the window to open it. A fly buzzed angrily in his face. He looked out, over the trees surrounding the gardens of Woodiscombe, to the uplands beyond. The fly brushed past him and flew out. Haines frowned and rubbed his eyes.

16

Cedric Demonstrates His Camera

The army stood as Cedric had left it. A black mass, evenly parted, as if a comb had run its teeth through a head of dense, springy hair. It was a windy day, but the strange new forest showed no sign of movement. Only the preserved trees by the boundary to the uplands bent slightly under its impact.

Haines took out his telescopic binoculars and peered through them at the waiting troops. He thought of the lines of crows, waiting on the telegraph wires as he made his way back from school, and found he was holding his breath as he had done then, dreading and half wishing the sudden clatter of movement, the flap of papery wings as they dived down around him. But he gazed on and the army remained still.

An arm circled Haines's waist. He let out his breath

too quickly and coughed. Cedric's face was parallel with his own, looking out at the regimented crowd.

"Amazing sight, isn't it? Those are my men, Mr. Haines. And women and children, I might add. At a signal from me they attack. What do you think of that?"

Haines occupied himself with the aerial, leaning from the window to pull the thin steel rod as far out as it would go. Fear made his hands thick and clumsy, like an alcoholic's. The aerial trembled at his repeated attempts to straighten it and he coughed again to hide his irritation. Cedric laughed quietly.

"Before you transmit, Haines, hadn't we better decide what to do with those troops? They could engulf us at any moment, you know. And they're all over England by now. The Government hasn't a leg to stand on, so to speak, and nowhere to put a leg down if it had one. I may add that all this happened purely accidentally. The fault of my past career, you could say. For some reason the people seem to think I'm Hitler. Well, I agree I was good in the part—"

"There's no proof whatsoever that—that a crowd like that exists anywhere but here," Haines said. In his attempt to recover his by now so easily threatened composure, he had pressed the volume button on his concealed transistor and a flood of muddled notes boomed out via the aerial into the garden below. A slight tremor ran through the army; with a curse Haines pounded at his tie to procure silence. An angry buzzing rose from the region of his chest.

"I have with me a small screen," Cedric said. "Allow me to demonstrate to you." He flipped open a pre-Revolutionary suitcase—pigskin, with *CB* in gold letters on the side—and pulled out an opaque oblong of concave plastic. With the rapid, confident movements of an inventor-cum-engineer (and artist and scientist, the now-forbidden Leonardo of the age) he fixed the screen to the aerial and depressed a knob that said Picture. Reluctantly, Haines looked on.

At first the screen showed nothing but confusion. Whirling gray blobs resembling caviar danced along vague ridges. Haines's lip curled. Then the blobs quieted, the lines straightened out. Violent color flooded the picture, turning the lines red and the increasingly human blobs a piercing shade of blue. In the background green hills rolled gently, as if photographed from a ship.

"The Lake District!" Haines knew the beauty spots of England from the geography films of his youth. "And an Army—"

"I only regret the hand-held effect," said Cedric. He twiddled the knob and the ocean, mauve and indigo and pale blue in the shallows, erased the lines of waiting troops in the north. Haines, despite himself, peered at the screen for a recognizable landmark. A band of white bisected the picture. Along it, blurred to begin with, then coming sharply into focus, stood regiments of black specks. The soft marine colors swirled around them.

"The white cliffs!" Haines whistled, setting up a whine from the half-disconnected bug under his tiepin. "So they're there too!"

"So far," Cedric, complained, "I have not been able to choose black-and-white and not color when I want to. But I dare say that will come."

He moved the knob slowly, allowing the armies to form at Gloucester and Birmingham before sweeping them away again with a flick of the wrist. "More troops than even I imagined," he confided to Haines. "Now what do you say?"

Haines sat down on the floor. Playing for time, he brushed the dead flies from under his silk trousers and laid them out in little piles on the dusty floorboards. Visions of revolutions rose before him: the French, which he saw in red, white, and blue, with the blood splashing from the guillotine baskets onto vermilion streets, an azure sky overhead; the Russian, all gray with the snow turned to gray slush and the massacred czar in an iron-gray basement, his grizzled head blown open against dirty white tiles; the recent one, in which he had participated, in the muddy English colors of lawn-green and suburban brick.

It was a long time since he had remembered so vividly the flat, overcast summer of his Government's coming to power—the arrests muffled in the leafy avenues, the dark office blocks where he had received his promotion. And now there was to be another!

Haines saw it in the false, plastic colors of Cedric's screen. It was unbearable. He made regiments of the dead flies, lining them up opposite Cedric and scraping together trenches made of dust.

"They won't do you much good," Cedric said. He gave a good-natured laugh. "You must admit now, Haines, that this little charade for the tourists is already out of date. What an earth is the point of trying to persuade me to murder poor old Jules when the diamond you carry in your pocket will feed and arm the troops and carry us to victory?"

"Victory?"

Haines saw his own murder, the diamond pillaged from his inner pocket, the end of law and order in the country which he loved and served. He jumped to his feet.

"I have no reason to believe your pretty pictures! A few men—a crowd—have collected on the uplands, exicted by your arrival. But you will obey orders, Mr. Brown, and follow instructions!"

"And the diamond? You promised to give it to Miss Pontoon, Haines. And take a cut yourself. Do you think your superiors will be impressed when they hear that?"

Haines pulled the recorder-transmitter from under his tie. Before speaking into the tiny microphone he glanced scornfully at Cedric.

"Do you imagine I had any intention of keeping the diamond, or allowing Miss Pontoon to keep it?

My presentation of the valuable stone to the Government takes place after the murder, when I have done my job with conscientious precision. They will be delighted. I have no doubt of that."

Haines blew into the pin-sized grill of his mouthpiece. Cedric pulled open his suitcase again.

"Allow me!"

With deft fingers he unfurled a strange contraption, which, once extended to its full length, he set on a tripod by the window.

"If you're determined to go ahead with your ridiculous plans, you might as well have a good microphone. A historic microphone, I might say. But you will regret this, Haines. You will regret it!"

Haines gasped. The recorder gasped back at him, filling the musty attic with a long, ghostly sigh. But Haines seemed oblivious to the fact that he was now on the air, recording direct to headquarters at Woodisford.

"That's the microphone that was designed for Lenin's speeches!" he cried.

The words boomed in echo, then snaked up the aerial to reach the ears of the waiting officials. Haines clapped a hand—too late!—over his mouth.

"How interesting that you should know that," Cedric remarked. "I don't think your bosses will appreciate your knowledge of an alien revolution, do you, Haines? But you are going ahead, I see. Go ahead, then."

Sweat stood out on Haines's brow as he transmitted his requests into his own State-supplied microphone. The bizarre 1917 invention, like a giant science-fiction insect, stood between him and the window and he stumbled against it twice as he spoke.

> "NEED TWENTY WEDDING GUESTS MARRIAGE JULES TANNER AND BESSY PONTOON STOP MARRIAGE PREVENTS PONTOON COMMITTING MURDER HOLDING APPROVED SUSPECT CEDRIC BROWN HERE STOP SEND DORA VIOLET EX ARMY OFFICER SIMON PETWORTH AND OTHERS FROM NEO RICH QUARTER AS SUSPECTS ROGER OUT HAINES,"

he stammered into the apparatus. Then he turned to Cedric once more.

"You're satisfied, I hope, Mr. Brown, that I have every intention of doing my duty?"

"So it seems." Cedric shrugged. "To tell the truth, Haines, I don't very much care what happens. It is more a question of the waste of human life. My men—as I am conceited enough to call them—could take over without the shedding of blood, if you cooperate. If you don't—"

Haines, silent and satisfied, packed away his equipment into his inner pocket and walked in a businesslike manner to the door.

"It's more a question of it being a waste of time

for you to try and remove—remove anything from my person," he said. "The resulting action taken by the Government would be swift and final, as I hope you understand."

"And if the Government loses the war? If you have to escape? Where will you run to?"

Haines cast his eyes in the direction of the ceiling. He permitted himself a skeptical smile.

Cedric burst out laughing.

"You can't go up there, you know, Haines. Your precious planets don't exist! All that money spent on space stations for the exploration of nothing! Don't imagine you can take off for some distant star if life becomes unpleasant for you here! There's nothing out there at all. Nothing!"

Haines opened the door and stepped cautiously down the steep stairs.

"Hogwash, Mr. Brown!" he called back over his shoulder.

17

The Impatience of the Bride

It was generally agreed, with the excitement of the wedding to come, that the Woodiscombe guests should that night eat dinner alone in their rooms. Sing shuffled along the wide passages and up and down the great oak staircase with trays: soufflé Grand Marnier this evening, after a *truite au bleu,* plunged live into each diner's individual porcelain saucepan; a tisane blended from the Elizabethan herb garden; a bunch of white grapes, the stalk delicately wrapped in damp absorbent cotton.

By the time the trays had been collected, evening had fallen outside the windows of the manor. The crowd was unusually quiet. Only the click of the metal birds as they strutted along the south terrace was audible.

Bessy paced her room, mother-of-pearl revolver in hand. The long, tarnished mirror in the closet elongated and slimmed her figure, giving the illusion of a walking pink satin dressing gown, angular shoulders rising like a clothes hanger from the softly pleated folds of the corsage. From time to time she stopped in front of it, and then dived behind the glass at the collection of Jules's mother's old dresses, pulling out and discarding the faded and sequined gowns of that lady's unremarkable youth. Furs dropped from under mothproof bags and made a dead zoo at her feet—fox, beaver, and chinchilla, each with a faint, lingering smell that brought back memories of suppers at famous restaurants, private views at the museum, tea with famous authors. Bessy blinked back her tears as she rummaged for a suitable bag for the wedding. The little gold envelope, with its half-used bottle of smelling salts inside, was too old-fashioned. A crocodile monster, as square and unforgiving as the jaw of the late Lady Tanner, would in no way complement the casual, older-woman-getting-married look at which Bessy was aiming. A canvas beach bag (a miniature bottle of gin inside) was obviously out of the question. Finally, a black grosgrain evening purse was selected, more for its anonymity than its beauty. A crumpled invitation tumbled from the silk lining when Bessy opened it: *The Countess of Faro Requests the Pleasure of Lady Tanner's Company at the Wedding of her daughter Bessy to Captain Flowers. R.S.V.P.*

Strange irony! That wedding, another wedding which had never taken place—and to Captain Flowers, dear Captain Flowers! And why had the presents gone back, unused, unloved, to their senders? Because of Jules, of course! Jules, who had ruined the fine, smooth path of her life. Whom she would now marry—or kill.

It occurred to Bessy, thickened though her features had become with nostalgic tears, her eyes crooked with the effort of summoning them, that it was time she made up her mind which it would be. Revenge was a purer, a nobler motive than sentimentality. As Medea she towered in the bedchamber, sending icy vibrations around the four-poster and the irritating bric-à-brac collected by her late near-mother-in-law; as Penelope, the patient, the waiting, she was little more than a figure of fun. Yet Bessy loved a wedding. Her shoulders sagged in anticipation of the lace veil, the garland of early syringa picked by a loving bridegroom from the garden. She eyed the revolver with distaste. If only Jules—here Bessy made up her mind, pulled the satin sash tighter around her waist, and strode to the door. If Jules—tonight—proving the marriage could have some meaning.. . .

Other voices counseled Bessy to remember the past, to extract some wisdom at least from the last time this wild passion had seized her. She paid no attention to them and set off in the direction of Jules's room. (Haines would note later that she carried the revolver with her, in Lady Tanner's black evening purse.)

18

A Moonlight Stroll

Cedric swallowed the last of the soufflé and left his room quietly, the padded shoulders of his Oriental robe lending him the air of a stealthy samurai as he stalked the passages and landings of Woodiscombe. Moonlight poured in through the windows and made obscene shadows of the nylon bell-skirts and climbing legs which straddled the south facade of the house. He was sad and tired, and everything he saw reflected his mood. The swords and lances in the famous Uccello painting (restored to its place by Sing in preparation for the wedding) glinted cruelly at him. Titian's head of John the Baptist lay despondent in a basin of blood. In the great naval battle scenes which once again lined the hall he heard the splinter of prow on hull, the firing cannons and the crackle of flames at sea. Pre-Raphaelite heroines, stretched out on their biers of flowers, were no more than corpses, their stern features drained of life by the wicked princes to whom they had entrusted themselves. A bronze warrior, spear in hand, bore down on him in the vestibule. He sighed—so many reminders of the holocaust to come—and let himself out of the front door onto the gravel drive.

The garden was lighted theatrically by the moon. Cedric had performed the necessary eye operation on himself before leaving his retreat, and he gazed up into an otherwise empty, starless sky. Sometimes, he reflected bitterly, discoveries such as his were more of a pity than a contribution to progress. He missed the Great Bear, and the false brightness of Venus, and the secure knowledge that galaxy upon galaxy of unguessable worlds spun out there in the blackness. Then he felt boredom at the banality of his regret, and he danced the last few steps from the drive to the ancient yew walk. The brittle, lopsided figure of Fred Astaire animated for a moment the mournful avenue, with its pale statues on stands, and long grass which never lost the dew. A pheasant rose with a clatter from the hazelnut bower at the far end of the walk. Cedric snapped off a bough from a thick tree, then tossed it away. It only served as a reminder of past bloodshed, of the soldiers, stunted men, who had plucked the yew for bows at the battle of Crécy. Unarmed, he wandered on.

There was little doubt in Cedric's mind that the

ludicrous Haines had contacted his superiors by now and reported the existence of the menacing army that was advancing over the uplands to Stonehenge and beyond. If, of course, they hadn't noticed it themselves . . . But as Cedric knew, once bureaucrats got into power, they lost the faculty of eyesight. Probably they had sensed for some time that all was not well in the area, and had postponed an actual investigation, promising that at the slightest hint of an uprising troops would be sent in to crush it. Now the uprising was imminent—or was it? At the lack of a signal from Cedric, would the armies melt away? Further, how many of the men who had sprung to life on his screen swore allegiance to him (or Hitler, or whoever they thought their leader was) and how many to the Government? His invention was brilliant, but it failed to tell him the one thing he wanted to know. Cedric smiled in resignation, stepped out of the yew walk and into the full, moonlit radiance of the old lawn. If he wondered what failure of will led him to his decision of inaction, he didn't wonder long. After all these years, he had no intention of playing the part of trigger in the biggest explosion the country had ever known. And he sensed that somewhere—here in the garden—he would find the answer to his long, enigmatic life.

Fifty feet away, behind the statue of Henry James, a figure flitted, then disappeared. Cedric felt a pang of fear. But why should he play the part of Polonius to Jules's Hamlet? Why should he end ignominiously on home-movie screens in Australia and New Zealand?

As a final joke he assumed the personality of Jules, and crossed the lawn.

19

The Sound of a Shot

Jules, highly pleased with himself, lay in white, monogrammed pajamas on his circular bed. Mirrors surrounded him, throwing back a hundred bottles of gold Sauterne on the table by his elbow; an unending procession of glass goblets marched away from him into the bright recesses of his room.

He stroked his silk sheets, thinking with satisfaction of the indefinite lease of life that lay ahead—yet not allowing himself to consider this too much, as a kind of irritation at life always seemed to succeed these particular thoughts. The present, the immediate future was what counted—his wedding, how enjoyable that would be!—all the old friends here again—the best of the herbaceous borders in bloom and the glass shrubs a heavenly blue from the cloudless sky. Good, sensible Haines!

Jules reflected happily that there was something of the fairy-story happy ending in all this: Haines wanted the diamond, and he should have it (Bessy would be easily satisfied with the lesser jewels from the cellar); Jules wanted a little longer in his miraculous sanctuary; Bessy wanted—well, perhaps it wasn't so bad, at his age, to be wanted by a fine woman like Bessy.

Jules patted at one of his myriad mirror heads and watched a vain smile run around the glassed walls of the room. He lay flat and stared up at his own eyes, once twin pools of blue, as they looked down at him. He was shortsighted now and a blurred, unshaven face hung, neckless, above his: a face like a monster's, without dignity or meaning. But Jules refused to permit this apparition to spoil his mood. He closed his eyes and drifted off into a light sleep.

Bessy opened the door noiselessly and crept over the massed polar bear skins to the great bed. She saw the Jules of the past, the beautiful young man who had floated, hair Ophelia-spread, on the current of the slow-moving river at Woodiscombe. It was a romantic moment; ancient dance tunes returned to her, solemn church music and the joyous peal of wedding bells filled her ears. So soon—to be hers! She bent down and pressed the red outline of her mouth on Jules's wrinkled cheek.

Jules awakened with a shriek. The phantoms he had thought gone forever swarmed about the foot of his bed—Sir Clovis, laughing and holding his cane high,

David, shabby and doleful in the splendor of the room, Bessy Pontoon in a satin gown which thrust her breasts like missiles at his vulnerable body. He rolled from the sheets, landed on a collection of French glass paperweights and, sliding and hobbling, dashed for the door. Sir Clovis and David vanished as he lunged at them. Only Bessy followed, her mouth a scarlet cavern of desire and rage.

A few paces ahead, encumbered by the balls of glass (packed with colored sands and stiff, dried flowers, skidding under his feet as he ran), Jules reached the mirrored shutters to the garden door, gasped once at his hideous face and rabbit eyes, fought his way out into the cool night air.

A shot rang out. Birds flew from the high elms and away over the uplands. A murmur ran through the waiting army, then subsided. Sing, awakened from his sleep in the pantry, shuffled onto the moonlit lawn.

20

The Change in Haines

The shot went unnoticed by Haines, who was busy constructing clues in his room.

First a scenario was needed, to be conveyed via earphones to the touring public. Haines stacked his little packages of fingerprint powder and lipstick-stained cigarette ends to one side of the desk and wrote quickly and efficiently on the Woodiscombe writing paper.

THE LAST COUNTRY HOUSE MURDER

Here, the morning room, the site of Mr. Jules Tanner's proposal to Miss Bessy Pontoon. A suitable room ladies and gentlemen—note the paintings: "Marriage at Cana" by Rubens, "The Odalisque" by Ingres, Hogarth's "Rake's Progress" just visible there through the door in Mr. Tanner's study, a reminder of bachelor days now forgotten, and a good thing too. (Pause for laughter.) Miss Pontoon accepted his proposal, but we must not count her out altogether. At Mr. Tanner's death, in pre-Revolutionary law, she stands to inherit all these magnificent possessions, this lovely country seat, and the famous Woodiscombe gardens. And we all know that ladies like Miss Pontoon are hardly aware that a Revolution took place at all! (Pause for more laughter.)

This, ladies and gentlemen, is the billiard room. Note the brightly colored balls and costly green baize. It was here that Mr. Cedric Brown attempted to blackmail Mr. Tanner, saying that he would reveal the unsavory secrets of Mr. Tanner's past to his bride if Mr. Tanner did not hand over to him the world-famous diamond (replica in glass case on north wall; original presented to the Government by Mr. Haines at the completion of the case). Mr. Tanner refused and further intimated that he had hidden the diamond in a place where Mr. Brown would never find it. We now go through to the Shell Room—shells arranged in a design by the late Lady Tanner—where Mr. Brown broke down and confessed to Mr. Tanner that he had always been in love with Bessy Pontoon and could not allow the marriage to take place. Note broken ashtray, hurled by Mr. Brown at the wall when Mr. Tanner replied he had every intention of going ahead with his marriage.

Haines paused here, removed the diamond from his pocket and laid it in front of him on the embossed leather surface of the table. He felt sure enough of himself now—and he had been sorely tried, by the stone itself, by Cedric's cunning pictures, but all these temptations he had resisted—to continue his reconstruction of the murder, with it gleaming in front of him. As if in obedience to its superior strength, the lights in the gloomy bedroom dimmed and the diamond shone brightly, casting its sharp rays over the paper. Unperturbed, Haines wrote on.

We are now in the great hall, awaiting the arrival of the wedding guests. There are closed-circuit screens above the portrait of the First Earl of Woodiscombe by Van Dyck, set into the paneling on the west wall. First come Dora and Violet, the famous Siamese twins who between them inherited three million pounds old sterling and spent it all on a party, roofing over Hyde Park in its entirety and employing no less than forty bands to play for three days and nights on real gold bandstands. (Pause for gasping.) As you can see, Dora and Violet both hold a grudge against Mr. Tanner. The story goes that they begged him for asylum at the time of the Revolution and he refused to let them into the house. This after his full enjoyment of their hospitality, which consisted of bringing an assortment of wild animals to the party and letting them loose in the mile-by-mile-and-a-half refreshment tent. They took no action against him at the time, but expected help in their hour of need. (Pause for disapproval.) So we will watch the movements, or perhaps I should say "movement," in the singular, of this aggrieved couple.

This is Simon Petworth, and we move now to the gun room—mind the fourteenth-century step there, ladies—where Mr. Tanner invited Simon Petworth to a duel after Mr. Petworth's allegation that Mr. Tanner cheated at cards. Pictures of dead game by the famous Dutch artist Van Offel. It was subsequently discovered that Mr. Petworth was a cheat and mountebank himself, and that he had been planning to do Mr. Tanner out of his home and fortune at the turn of a duplicated two of spades. Mr. Tanner unveiled the mystery, and ever since that day Simon Petworth has been set on only one thing—the murder of Mr. Jules Tanner. (Pause for low buzz.)

The other wedding guests do not require your

particular attention. We are now standing in the chapel where the Archbishop of Canterbury was assassinated by Samuel Beckett, if you can cast your minds back to that period in your history books. For many a long day nothing as splendid or as doomed has taken place in this once-hallowed spot: to mark the anniversary of the end of the Catholic Church, the marriage service between Bessy Pontoon and Jules Tanner was performed in Latin (translations in four languages available from pew phones) and . . . ladies and gentlemen, here comes the bride! Screen above altar and on baroque stone tomb belonging to the third Earl of Woodiscombe. In the front row of the congregation is Lady Clorinda, whose scrap-books made the last great auction sale landmark—£405,984 for the collection of photographs of herself and her family—two days before our present Government put an end to speculation in art. (Pause for interested murmur.)

And now we pass through to the library. No pushing past the rope, please. The effigy of Jules Tanner which you see lying on the Aubusson carpet was made by Kenilworth Plastics Ltd. and portrays Mr. Tanner in his youth. The actual body, of course, is buried in the family vault, which we shall be visiting later. Mr. Tanner was shot through the chest, as you can see. There are

> many guns to choose from at Woodiscombe, and quite a few people with a good motive for shooting him. We hope you have been using your eyes, ladies and gentlemen, on this tour. Today's winner receives a souvenir miniature of the body, cast in reinforced styrofoam by Hepton Modern Artworks. On your marks, get set, fifteen minutes to solve the Woodiscombe murder mystery!

Haines wiped his brow with his Lord Peter Wimsey silk handkerchief and sat back in his chair. A cunning trail would lead the tourists to Jules and Bessy's nuptial chamber, out to the sunken garden where Dora, separated from Violet at last, was practicing at clay-pigeon shooting and telling everyone she was Violet and had just seen Dora shoot Jules in the morning room (all this on carefully placed closed-circuit screens, of course, and fresh clues put down every day); then onto the billiard room, where a slender gun disguised as a cue awaited the hand of Cedric. Suspicious-looking drinks mixed by Bessy for Jules were placed in the drawing room, and powder for forensic testing. A mock duel between Simon Petworth and Jules provided a suitable red herring. Finally, Cedric's prints were found on the cue, and the bullet wound in the plastic body was shown to match the firearm. Cedric was arrested and led away.

But there was still much to be done! The silence from the crowds on the uplands had had a calming effect on Haines, and he went with quiet precision about his tasks. Cedric's mad rantings seemed already to belong to another age. No doubt the people had felt inclined, to pass the time perhaps or give themselves the illusion of organization, to make a formation resembling that of an army. How strange that Haines should have believed in their strength, when it was so obvious—had been so obvious from the very start—that the Government was unbeatable, and rightly so. How nearly he had allowed the diamond to exert its fateful influence! And, though he disliked to admit it now, how close he had been to joining Cedric's ramshackle troops and presenting them with the stone! At least, Haines reflected, if he had considered cheating his superiors at all, he might as well have fled to the other side of the world with it. His behavior demonstrated amply that he was an obedient and trustworthy man.

The bug on Haines's chest gave a low bleep. Frowning, Haines connected the transistor to the aerial and waited. A message from headquarters? If they should come now and see the unsuspected diamond lying on the table, accuse him unjustly of embezzlement, arrest him just as his moment of glory was at hand—

"WOODISFORD HEADQUARTERS TO HAINES," a voice

growled from the box. Haines stood to attention and saluted.

"Haines reporting," he said anxiously.

> EXTERIOR CIRCUMSTANCES PROHIBIT CEDRIC BROWN AS MURDERER STOP THIS MAN MUST ON NO ACCOUNT ACHIEVE FURTHER NOTORIETY BESSY PONTOON NOW PERFORMS FUNCTION ROGER OUT.

That was all. Haines waited, listening to the faint buzz from the transistor and the ominous silence from the crowd beyond the gates of Woodiscombe. Then, hardly conscious of his movements, he disconnected the equipment and stowed it away again.

So it was true! Cedric's Revolution was on the point of happening!

Haines scooped the diamond into his pocket and ran breathlessly through the darkened house in search of his new master.

21

Bessy, Haines, and the Diamond

Dawn showed a pale gray at the tops of the elms, making the rooks' nests stand out against the sky like black bundles. The flock of metal flamingos, their mechanism reactivated at the waning of the moon, were beginning to strut and peck along the sanded terrace, when Haines stumbled out into the garden, stood arms outstretched in the center of the lawn and called out for Cedric in the loudest voice he could muster.

There was no answer, only the distant splash from the waterfall garden and Bessy's muffled sobs (Haines did not yet know of Bessy's grief, and thought she was one of the streams that ran down to the waterfall, humped by Japanese bridges). There was no sign of anyone in the house either. Haines had run from room to room, taking in only subliminally the chaos of Jules's bedroom, the splintered, still-rolling paperweights, the clothes lying like unswept leaves in the room that had once been Lady Tanner's.

Cedric's neat bachelor quarters had revealed nothing, except that the bed had not been slept in that night. The room might not have known an occupant since the days of moustached young men, not so young as they appeared, who came to stay with Sir Clovis and sat up all night drinking his brandy. Even the pantry, where Sing could usually be counted on to be lying on his shelf, surrounded by exotic spices and sacks of flour and rice, was empty and abandoned.

Haines circled the great lawn, while the moon went down behind the trees and a thin gray light, impossible to see by but making the eyes strain in an effort to remember the light of day, crept slowly into its place. A blur beneath the cedar turned out to be nothing more than a garden bench. The hammock swung like a shroud between two invisible trees.

"Mr. Haines!"

Haines started, feeling a cold current of fear trickle from his shoulders to the base of his spine. He swung around, his fist closed on the diamond.

"Mr. Haines—it's me—Bessy!"

A white orb hung suspended in the air a few feet away. Haines shrank back as it swam toward him, gradually attaching itself to the ground by means of a shadowy body and trailing pale-colored gown. An icy hand fastened on his.

"Look, Mr. Haines—just look what I've done! Over there!"

Haines was conscious of feeling, as he followed the trembling and haunted Bessy across the lawn, a surge of almost welcome resignation and defeat. There had been too many things to cope with in the last two days: the magnetic power of the diamond; the terrible, corrupting atmosphere of Woodiscombe; an impending war; and, worst of all for the nerves, a total change of allegiance from the Department he had served so long to a state of near-idolatry for an unknown, and possibly mad, genius. Something in him greeted the prone, stiff body lying in the dew outside the French windows with a kind of ironical joy—it was no longer his responsibility if the murder case was bungled; how could he be blamed for a single mistake when there was a general massacre to come? Anxiety lifted from him; mentally he disassociated himself from the whole business; finally he turned to Bessy and smiled. Yet he knew at the same time that these were nothing more than the symptoms of shock. He must escape—either alone or with Cedric. For the time his brain refused to allow him to think seriously about the matter, and he postured, seeing himself now as a ludicrous parody of a man, on the lawn beside the equally unimportant corpse.

"So you murdered Jules Tanner, Miss Pontoon?"

The dense grayness of the light had lifted a little, and Bessy's haggard features could now be seen more clearly. Her sobbing, Haines thought distantly, sounded like a hen clucking before it lays an egg.

"So awful—only wanted to—don't know what came over me, Mr. Haines. And why on earth—did I—go to his room carrying this?"

The mother-of-pearl revolver lay in the daisies at her feet. Haines stooped down and retrieved it, careful even now to preserve the fingerprints. He toyed with the idea of confiding in Bessy, explaining that the murder was quite unnecessary, taking her to the gates and showing her the lines of troops; then decided against it for the time being. A numb smile stood out on his face.

"And now there won't be a wedding!" Bessy moaned. "I can't bear it!"

"Where is Sing, Miss Pontoon?"

"Sing? He ran away, Mr. Haines! I saw him climb a tree up there by the road and jump over onto the uplands." Bessy's lacquered nails dug deeper. "There's something happening, isn't there, Mr. Haines? Please tell me! What is it?"

Haines's mind clicked into order. Day spread through the garden, restoring the vague outline of the west wing to its usual place, rubbing out the pools of shadow that had extended it into flower beds and lawn. A rattle—like the sound of presenting arms in some faraway parade—came over the tops of the trees.

"What was *that?*" cried Bessy.

Haines stepped over the corpse and went through the open French window into the house. He picked a dust sheet from a long-neglected sofa and returned with it. Carefully he draped it over the premature body.

"That is Mr. Cedric Brown's army," he replied. He spoke in a new, quiet tone which Bessy seemed to find even more disturbing. She fell on her knees on the wet grass and her sobs turned to a high, soft scream. Haines pulled her up again.

"This is no time for emotion, Miss Pontoon. We have to find Cedric, and quickly. First—if you wouldn't mind taking the legs, Miss Pontoon—that's right. We will place the body in the library."

With his new awareness of himself, Haines smiled grimly at his last words. He was a cautious man, certainly; perhaps even a coward. If Cedric lost, was defeated—then there was still a body waiting for the tourists. Haines marveled at his pragmatic turn of mind.

"And where is Cedric, Miss Pontoon?"

Together they had covered the chalk mark on the carpet with the bundled body of the murdered man. Haines, despite himself, felt a certain pride at a mission accomplished. Then he turned severely to Bessy and repeated his question.

"Cedric? I've no idea, Mr. Haines. What do you mean, that's his army? I don't understand! Please don't leave me alone here!"

If he has gone to join them without me . . . Haines mused. He said aloud, "Did you know Mr. Brown was a great leader, a great scientist, Miss Pontoon? That he has discovered the nonexistence of the universe?"

"What? Don't be silly, Mr. Haines." Bessy recovered some of her old vigor at this suggestion. "Of course there's a universe out there. It must have been one of Cedric's jokes. He was a great practical joker in the old days, you know." She heaved a sigh. "Well, those days are truly over now that poor Jules is dead. I can't think why I—"

Another fit of sobbing filled the room. Haines pulled impatiently at his inner pocket. Maybe, with his aerial, he would be able to pick Cedric up somewhere, hear the beloved voice on some distant battlefield. He remembered with reverence the little homemade screen on which he had been shown the symbols of his leader's power. If only he had trusted his eyes then!

The diamond fell out of his pocket and rolled along the floor. Bessy was saying impatiently, "You don't need to find Cedric to do the murder now, Mr. Haines. Surely you've grasped that. I don't believe in these armies of his at all!"

The sobs which followed this statement ended abruptly. A silence fell between Bessy and Haines as the diamond came to rest on the carpet by the long mirror. For a time they both stared at it; then, finally, their eyes met.

The sun rose over the trees by the Woodiscombe gates. As the first shaft came in through the library windows, the diamond shone and sparkled and sent its rays of pure light around the room—like a star fallen onto a field of lilies bound by scarlet and gold thread.

22

The Wedding

The chapel, decorated the day before by Sing and Jules, was heavy with the fragrance of syringa and moss roses. It was a fine day for the wedding, and the guests wore an assortment of floral hats and herbaceous dresses which lent a bucolic, festive air to the occasion. Top hats sat beside their owners in the pews reserved for the oldest friends of Jules and Bessy.

Outside on the lawn, the more privileged tourists picnicked to the accompaniment of an operatic medley. The lane was blocked with the buses of those who had found themselves unable to pay five thousand dollars admission to Murder Manor, as Woodiscombe was now popularly called. Nevertheless, closed-circuit TV in the interior of the vehicles provided everything but mood. There was a pleasant feeling of anticipation in the air; and it was considered a typical example of British courtesy that the people lined up on the uplands should be standing permanently to attention.

"I guess we should ask them to relax," said Mr. Irving. (He and his wife were part of the bus-viewing party; Mrs. Latham and Mrs. Wrexham had paid up and were even now sitting on the lawn.) "They'll be pretty tired by the end of the day." Mr. Irving's claustrophobic tendencies had grown since the beginning of the tour, and he found the lines of motionless men oppressive.

"British soldiers never die," Mrs. Irving snapped at him. Then she sat forward in her seat with pleasure as a deafening blast of Mendelssohn filled the bus. "Here comes the bride!" she reminded her husband. "I'm almost feeling sad there has to be a murder after this."

A rumor was running through the guests in the chapel. Its insigator was Lady Clorinda Foxe, who had brought her camera to record the romantic event for her album. On peering through the ancient but still accurate lens she had seen a face—a strange face, a slightly sinister face even—reflected in the Tanner Silver Chalice on the altar. She nudged Dora, her neighbor, whose nudge was naturally transferred to her twin Violet and thence to the rest of the once-distinguished congregation. A soft ripple of speculation followed.

"I agree it's not very like Jules from behind," Simon

Petworth hissed into the ear trumpet of the former choreographer, Sir Miles Nash. "Unless the fellow's shrunk a bit since I last saw him."

"Probably you took a few inches off him in that duel," Lady Clorinda giggled from her second-row pew. "Do you remember, Simon?"

The sounds of *Lohengrin* swelled out through the chapel and the whispers were submerged. A murmur of regulation envy and appreciation went out to meet the bride, who was walking slowly up the aisle on the arm of her cousin, Lord Canasta. Under the thick white veil, recognizable features could dimly be perceived. Lady Clorinda noisily took a flash picture.

"Isn't she lovely?" Mrs. Latham cried, staring up at the screen suspended from the great cedar on the lawn. "Sometimes, you know, I wish we hadn't done away with weddings altogether!"

"We always felt it was because no one wanted to marry women like you," Mrs. Wrexham said sharply. "You people put the world where it is today."

"Where it is a more equal place," said Mrs. Latham. "With the end of male chauvinism we have for the first time the possibility of peace and harmony."

"I can't see any sign of it," Mrs. Wrexham said as the courier came toward them with a request to keep quiet. "After this wedding, for instance, the bride is going to murder the groom. I don't call that progress!"

The courier smiled coyly at the ladies, placing his gloved finger to his lips.

"Silence! If you please! We don't know yet, Mrs. Wrexham, that Mr. Tanner will be murdered by his bride, do we?"

"Who else is there?" Mrs. Wrexham replied in a bored, sulky voice. She was already regretting the outlay of five thousand dollars, which would otherwise have bought her a complete tour of the whisky distilleries of Scotland.

Mrs. Latham had jumped to her feet and was waving excitedly at the screen.

"Something's gone wrong with the wedding! Look, Molly! Everyone's got up from their seats—they're swarming about everywhere—has he been murdered in *church*? Really!" (Mrs. Latham had thrown off a passionate religious temperament as a child, and was easily shocked.)

23

The Impediment

Haines stood facing the altar. He was very conscious of the whispering behind him, the inevitable speculation that this wasn't Jules at all, but some impostor; and he needed all the support he could get from the new inner voice that had been born in him with the rising of the sun that morning.

Luckily, the voice didn't fail him. The miracle of the diamond was too recent for that, the dawning of love between Bessy and himself too overpowering to be forgotten or swept aside by agitation from the outside world. It mattered not at all, now, that the world he had once helped to bring into being was on the point of being destroyed. He no longer cared for the whereabouts of Cedric, or whether his erstwhile masters were in fact stronger than the rebellious troops.

For the first time in his life Haines had no need of a leader. With the woman he loved at his side, he could go through life alone—if there was any life left to him, he could fend for himself. It was a strange and thrilling feeling.

The organ music grew louder, and the elderly, fashionable vicar imported from London looked anxiously up the aisle at the symptoms of increasing restlessness in the congregation. It was a long time since he had conducted a marriage ceremony. Was all this talking and pointing the thing nowadays? He was sorry, too, that no best man had been provided. The groom had intimated that he had the ring himself. Did that really matter? It was so hard to know what was blasphemy and what was unimportant.

Bessy reached Haines's side in a heavenly crescendo. Haines turned his head very slightly, as grooms were allowed to do, and smiled tenderly at the almost concealed face behind Lady Tanner's veil. He thought of the magic of the diamond, and the moment their souls had been flooded with its radiance in the library, and the hurried lovers' plans to escape together after the service on a permanent and blissful honeymoon. If only it would come true! But Haines knew by now that faith was all that counted, and that he must not think of Cedric's angry shock troops, or of possible imprisonment at Woodisford. He must think of Bessy, and of their future together.

The sacred moment was approaching. Oblivious to the squeaks of surprise and disapproval, Haines pulled the diamond from his pocket once more. Bessy stretched out a hasty finger, but it seemed almost impossible that a human hand would have the strength to support so huge a stone. In its dancing light their eyes met. Bessy, behind the veil, was smiling. The vicar's voice droned on.

". . . any known impediment . . ."

There was a clatter at the back of the chapel. The door was thrown open, and then came a scream of rage which threw the wedding guests into uproar.

"I object! There is indeed an impediment! That's the wrong man!"

Haines had to turn now, to grasp at Bessy as she began to run back along the aisle, to follow, stumbling after her, and implore her to stay with him.

Bessy's sobs came loud and muffled in reply. Lady Clorinda barred Haines's path with strong arms. Simon Petworth kicked at him. He fell back on the altar, breathless and defeated.

"Jules! Jules!" Bessy cried. "How can you be here? I killed you last night!"

(In the coach, Mrs. Irving sighed with excitement. Mr. Irving's eyes were closed in distress. "It's a more tricky ending than I imagined," she told the other viewers.)

Jules pushed his way through the crowd to stand

over Haines. His hair was disheveled and he was wearing an Oriental robe.

"Everyone to the house!" he shouted over the pandemonium. "And you, Mr. Haines, are going to come with me!"

The guests fell back as Jules and Haines left the chapel and crossed the few feet of lawn which separated it from the house. A cheer went up from the tourists.

24

Tourists Disappointed

Cedric had finally abandoned the personality of Jules and had returned, in the repose of death, to being himself. His face looked tired and disappointed as Jules pulled back the sheet. Perhaps the joke had seemed less funny at the last minute, when the flitting figure on the lawn had proved to be Bessy with a gun. Possibly he had felt a sudden pang of regret as he died, at having made the universe into a play on words The diamond, the only star he had continued to see till the end, was held by Jules now. Cedric's eyes stared blankly up at it from the floor.

"So, ladies and gentlemen," Jules said. "It seems that I have to play the part of detective after all. Our friend Mr. Haines here has bungled things a little, I'm afraid. But I hope we are all charitable enough to allow the happy couple to elope, as they had intended." He turned to Bessy, who was sitting dejectedly on the floor. (Haines was beside her, his head bowed; from time to time Dora and Violet wandered into him, in their strange quadruped peregrinations about the library.) Jules smiled, and Bessy wept again, dabbing at her red eyes with the torn veil.

"No, my dear Bessy, you will have to go without a dowry." Jules held the diamond high, so that the midday sun was thrown in prisms of blinding light around the corners of the high room. "I had forgotten what a beautiful stone this was, I must confess. Well, Mr. Haines, are you ready for your honeymoon now?"

"I can't understand what's going on," Mrs. Irving complained to her sleeping husband. "Hey!" She leant forward suddenly and peered out at the road. "The police seem to be trying to get through here, Irving. I thought this was a Scenic Area, only tourist traffic allowed here. And on the day of the murder, too!"

"Seems they killed the wrong man," the woman behind Mrs. Irving said. "I think it's all a bit of a letdown, personally."

On the lawn, Mrs. Latham heard police sirens and nodded wisely to Mrs. Wrexham.

"They're going to arrest her now, I suppose. Pity the picture keeps getting cluttered with all those hats, though. I've lost the plot, I think. Who got murdered?"

Mrs. Wrexham had said several times that she was

going to ask for her money back. Now, Mrs. Latham's obtuseness was proving the last straw.

"A man called Cedric Brown got murdered. By Jules Tanner's bride. Didn't you even grasp that?"

"Who's he?" demanded Mrs. Latham.

"The man she thought was Jules Tanner," Mrs. Wrexham said in disgust.

"What was the motive, then?"

Mrs. Wrexham rose with tired anger from her rug and stalked off to find the courier. "He was a man. Isn't that enough for you?" she called back over her shoulder. Whether the courier liked it or not, Mrs. Wrexham was going to insist on instant departure from Woodiscombe. The outing had been a flop, and if they hurried they could reach the *London by Night Show* in the fast bus. The bitter quarrel which ensued floated in through the library windows to the ears of the wedding guests. Sirens drowned it out a moment later. Haines hid his head between his knees and waited for the end.

"The police," Jules said gaily. "Mr. Haines, it seems likely that you will be charged with being an accessory after the fact, so we must say good-bye now. What a shame you and Bessy didn't have the energy to make a getaway while there was still time. Never mind! One must be brave!"

"I want a photograph of them together before they go," said Lady Clorinda. She swung her Leica in the direction of the downcast couple. "Please, Bessy, just a little smile for me!" she cried in the fake Cockney accent so loved by her circle in the past. "Say 'Cheese'!"

Haines leaped for the diamond. As he jumped, and the guests staggered back in amazement, a wild cheering from the buses broke out at this sudden piece of action in an otherwise slow-moving film. The police cars stopped at the gates of Woodiscombe, pressing down on their horns for someone to run out and let them in. The wail of the sirens started a corresponding cry from Jules's peacocks in the waterfall garden. The privileged tourists on the lawn ran forward to admit law and order as quickly as possible to the scene of near-chaos in the house. Footsteps sounded on the gravel drive.

The diamond, wrenched from Jules's hand, spun across the library like a meteor. A cry went up from the wedding guests and tourists alike as it made a perfect, brilliant rainbow in the high dome of the room, and came down like a ball of flame into the fireplace.

Fear succeeded astonishment. Reflected sun from the stone kindled the dry timber (a fire last laid in the room on the day of Sir Clovis's funeral); fire blazed suddenly out, belching from the sooty chimney into flowered hats and monocled faces. Black smoke poured out of the windows, choking Mrs. Latham as she ran for safety. A great metallic rattle sounded from the uplands.

Haines, gasping for breath by the damask curtains,

heard Cedric's words ringing in his ears: "At a signal from me they will attack . . . ," heard the rush of the troops as, like a flood of pent-up water, they swarmed over the uplands to Woodiscombe in answer to the vast column of smoke, and he fell on his knees and prayed. Boots mounted the stairs. Cedric's army poured over the lawn. The fighting outside the library was short and vicious. Victorious, the rebels trampled the tourists, suffocated the wedding guests, and overthrew the buses in their stampede for freedom and justice.

Haines had little time in which to think back over his life. He saw his father, with Jules's father's features incongruously superimposed; he felt the bitterness of failure and the longing for a quiet life at Woodiscombe with Bessy at his side. In his last fleeting thoughts he imagined himself to be both Jules and Cedric. Bessy, torn from his embrace by the flailing troops, lay crushed with Dora and Violet, her oldest friends.

25

The End

Jules spent several weeks clearing up the mess left by Cedric's army. He had had the sense to slip up the secret staircase from the library to his bedroom at the time of trouble, and thence to the attic, where he now slept and contemplated the garden in his waking hours. July had passed, and he felt bored at the prospect of August; the quality of light was bad in Wiltshire then, and most of the glass shrubs that had once reflected the clouds had been broken in the battle.

Sing was gone, too. One of the soldiers posted outside the chapel (now Cedric's shrine) came in the evenings and cooked him a meal. But Jules often said that he was seriously contemplating suicide.

"May is my favorite time of year," he told David

Makins in the long, lonely nights at the top of the manor. Sometimes he showed the young doctor the diamond. "If Mr. Haines had been wise enough to accept it as a bribe in the first place," he remarked, "things wouldn't have gone so wrong. I only wanted another week!"

Makins was sulky these days, and never answered.